Tales from the Portly Pixie

'Of Cabbages, Kings and Things'

Foolish talk leads to a fruitless hunt in the woods but a triumphant return to the place it all started from so that it could begin all over again

by

Roger Price

2nd. Edition February 2021

Originally published October 2011
In limited printed editions and as a Kindle download

Based on an original adventure from "The Portly Pixie Live Role Playing Centre"
With thanks to all those who made the stories different every time no matter how often they were told and the originals of the many characters featured herein

Chapter 8: Thwarted Escape

Gerald pressed himself hard against the stone wall of the corridor. Even though he was desperate to escape detection. He could feel the damp behind him. It was the slime on the wall eating through the lightweight black leather waistcoat he was wearing. "It'll be into the silk shirt next," he thought to himself, "Will I never learn?"

As he stood, trying to act like another piece of the wall, he looked carefully around him. He was surprised that he could see at all. He had thought he was in total darkness. Then he realised there was a dim light. He struggled to see where it was coming from. Finally he realised it was the same slime that even now was devouring his clothing. It was everywhere. It covered the walls. It dripped from the ceiling. It had gathered in pools at his feet and, even now, was flowing down his spine towards the small of his back. Everywhere he looked it glowed with a light of its own.

But he realised that he was making a big mistake. Looking closer he could see that it was the mosses and lichens of an unusual, distorted, nature that struggled for life within the slime in this harsh, underground, environment that were providing the faint illumination.

"Interesting - if you like plants!" came the unbidden thought.

There was a sudden noise to his left. Remembering that he had almost made a bigger mistake, Gerald struggled to make himself an even smaller part of the wall as he turned to look that way. His feet moved on something hard amid the slime on the corridor floor. It crunched, wetly, as if he had just stood on a snail. He was glad that he couldn't see what it was in the dim lichen light! But he could see that something - or someone - was coming down the corridor towards him.

Once more he became motionless. He listened more intently. He could hear the squelch of leather boots in whatever it was that flowed with a life of its own along the floor. He detected the clink of sword on stone as those who approached probed the sides of the tunnel seeking out concealed prey. And then one more piece of evidence confirmed the suspicion that had been growing in his mind. He heard voices.

"Why are we looking for just one of them? We've got the rest," whined one of the approaching shapes. "Because we've been told to by the boss" came another that spoke with authority. "Can't we say we tried and go back to the warmth of the fire?" the moaning voice came again with the general agreement of the rest of the half seen figures.

Gerald watched intently as the henchmen came towards him. Their noisy search of the corridor came to a sudden stop. He sensed their leader turning to inspect his troop by the light of the lantern he carried. Gerald listened as the answer was given: "Because the Boss would not like it. Now, shall we get on?" Once more the search party was coming Gerald's way.

"Time to go" Gerald thought and he began to inch his way along the wall. Looking back he could see that the searchers were coming closer. He speeded up a little, watching anxiously to see if he was making any headway.

Suddenly Gerald stopped dead in his crablike progress. His foot had come down on something slightly firmer amongst whatever it was on the floor. Through his soft leather boots Gerald tried to work out what it was. He failed and knew that he was going to have to look.

Looking downwards Gerald realised that his foot had come to rest on top of another. This one was inside a rather nice black leather boot with some red bits crafted into it, all finished off with white stitching. And there was a leg coming down into it. Gerald's eye slowly made its way upwards along the black linen of the trousers, over the finely crafted leather belt with gold inlay, rising across the padded and studded leather waistcoat, to finally reach the face of the owner of the boot.

Gerald could see the face clearly in the light of the approaching lantern. There was the short, well trimmed, jet black beard, the dark foreboding eyes with that hint of cunning and the slicked back hair revealing the tribal tattoo dominating the forehead. It wasn't a face that you were likely to forget.

This was Luther D'Eth, the most villainous bandit in the whole of Chouse. And that explained many things to Gerald - all be it too late to make any real difference to the current mission. This was the outlaw who had had the gall to capture the Arch Mage Mandrake in order to force him to be his ally. This was the thieving git who had masterminded the planned sacking of Sham by the renegade orc tribes. He'd even managed to kidnap Piper and was "persuading" him to create a fog to cover the attack when Gerald and his friends had once more saved the day. Yes, this was not a face - or a person - you were likely to forget.

Gerald had not forgotten him. And it was clear from the look in his eyes that Luther had not forgotten Gerald either. They were saying that he was about to eat a meal of cold revenge and Gerald was going to be the main course!

"Hallo Luther," Gerald said with more warmth than he felt.

"You weren't leaving us so soon?" came the icy cold reply.

Gerald paused before making any reply and, strangely, Luther gave him time to think, confident in his approaching men to carry the moment. Gerald was acutely aware of Luther's henchmen as well. Not only were their squelching and grumbling getting louder but the lantern was making it easier by the moment for Gerald to see Luther. It was not a pretty sight.

Gerald made up his mind and drew in a deep breath. Luther tilted his head slightly to one side in silent enquiry. He was asking himself if the witty response was going to be worth the wait. But Gerald said nothing. That was not the decision he had come to. He'd remembered that actions always speak louder than words.

With all his strength Gerald stamped down onto Luther's foot. It had the desired effect. Luther was painfully hurt and gave out a ear splitting yell of pain and frustration. He lifted the seemingly broken foot into his hands to massage some life back into it. And Gerald was off like a flash.

No more creeping around in the dark - now it was the time to make the last desperate attempt at escape. This was the moment to make the dash to seek the help he needed against the notorious enemy of the law. He wasn't sure which way he was going - but he was going that way as fast as possible. The footing was treacherous and in less desperate times would have added excitement to his wild flight into the dark maze of tunnels. But Gerald had only one thought as he struggled to keep his feet as he ran. He was not pleased and wished he had stayed in the inn.

Luther was not pleased either, hopping on his one good foot in the mire in the semi dark. His henchmen breathlessly arrived to identify the source of the blood curdling scream. They were amused by the sight that greeted them but tried not to show it. They stood, silently, subserviently, submissively, sinking slowly into the mire of the tunnel floor.

Finally Luther stopped his hopping and looked at his men without any real feeling of hope or expectation. A silence descended on the scene, broken only by the ever present plop of water from the tunnel roof. It was clear that Luther was going to have to break this stillness.

With his voice dripping with more sarcasm than the dripping water he asked "Well?"

"Err. Are you all right, boss?" replied his hopeless lieutenant, "Was it him?".

"Yes," Luther retorted, "He went that way." He pointed into the darkness that covered Gerald's flight. The henchmen peered in the indicated direction, trying to see the fleeing figure of their prey. The lieutenant even lifted his lantern a little bit higher as if it would help.

Luther was ready to bang his head against the moss covered and slimy wall in his frustration. He knew he had had to scrape the bottom of the criminal underworld barrel to recruit this lot but surely they knew what to do next. As the moments drew into minutes it became clear that nothing was going to happen. Luther gave vent to his frustration shouting "Get after him".

There was another unending pause as even this simple instruction bored its slow way into the sawdust of the brains for which it was intended. Luther could contain himself no longer. The next instruction came louder than the last: "Now!!" The very volume added wings to feet and the henchmen were rushing off into the dark.

Further along the tunnel Gerald had come to a squelchy full stop in front of a thick wooden, iron nail studded, door. Tentatively he turned the large, heavy, metal ring that served as a handle and pulled the door towards him. Nothing. He pushed with all his weight. Still nothing. The conclusion was obvious - it was locked. And there was nowhere else to go.

Sighing to himself, he sank to one knee in the ever present slime. He pulled out the lock picks from his waist band. Desperately he began to work on the large, rust stained, iron lock set into the body of the door. But no matter how he tried, the latches just would not respond to his attentions.

Gerald knew that time was running out because it was getting lighter where he worked. While this did make it easier to see what he was doing it also meant that his pursuers were getting closer. Very soon Gerald could hear their boots approaching along the swampy floor. The footsteps stopped and Gerald knew that it was too late.

With bowed head in seeming defeat he slowly rose to his feet. He turned to face his would be captors. He showed them his empty hands, having slipped the lock picks back into their hiding place. Sullen, angry, faces greeted his diffident, outwardly friendly, air. Gerald decided he was going to have to make the first move.

"Hi lads. Any chance we can talk this over?" he asked, more in hope than expectation. The response was a snarl as the henchmen continued their careful prowl towards their prey. Considering this Gerald muttered "I guess not, then", more to himself than expecting a reply. He readied himself for action. He decided that attack was still the best form of defence and threw himself at the largest of the henchmen.

A quick fist in the face, followed by a knee in the tender parts, and the first foe was down. The next one soon joined him after his head came into sharp contact with the thick wooden door. "This is going to be easy" Gerald thought to himself as he speedily despatched the third of the bandits in a similar style. But it wasn't to be that simple. Gerald was so busy dealing with the obvious that he overlooked the cautious.

The leader of this particular band of thugs had not risen to the high post of lantern carrier just because he had brawn and knew how to use it. He also had some brains and had found that using them came in handy from time to time too. Watching the ease with which his prey was dealing with his less cautious colleagues made him realise that this was one of those times to think before acting. Slowly the cogs turned and a plan of action popped into the mind of the thug. He was going to have to do something - and do it soon. Otherwise Gerald would escape again and Luther would not be pleased - again.

Slowly, carefully looking for a firmer section of slime on which to rest it, he placed the lantern on the floor. Carefully, keeping a wary eye on the unfolding action before him, he drew the iron banded stick out of his belt. Weighing it expertly in his hand he watched the fight, looking for an opening. When it came he didn't hesitate but brought the stick down sharply and firmly on the back of Gerald's head.

Gerald hadn't seen the stick wielding thug making his preparations but he felt the result. As the blackness of unconsciousness welled up inside him Gerald experienced a fleeting thought. He knew he had been struck by an expert. The blow had been delivered with a calculated force. It had been designed to make him insensible. A fraction harder and it would have cracked his skull. A fraction less and it would have only made him angry - very angry. Gerald's last thought as he sank face down into the slime was "No, I've been hit just right." The blackness claimed him before he had a chance to realise where his face now lay.

Relieved that their prey had nowhere to go, the bandits began attending to each other's wounds. Heads were rubbed and arms put back into joint. Their lantern carrying, stick wielding, leader looked on at these antics, wondering if any one of them but him had noticed that Gerald was slowly drowning in the mud. It became clear they hadn't and his contempt for his assistants became a little greater.

"Turn him over before he drowns," he barked. The order was greeted with blank, uncomprehending, looks. Pointing at the unconscious Gerald, he explained "Him. Now." Finally they jumped into action - well, more lumbered and limped - and Gerald was turned face up, saved from a slimy death. If it wasn't for the muck and filth on his face you could have been excused for thinking him asleep. The chief henchman contemplated his prize before ordering his crew to "bring him along". The bruised and battered bandits retraced their steps, dragging Gerald along by his ankles.

Gerald slowly came back to wakefulness. His first thought was "I don't remember ordering a mud bath" as he felt the sludge from the corridor floor move over his back, his neck, his head and his hair. Then recollection came flooding back. He knew - roughly - where he was and knew - vaguely - what was going on. His next thought was that he was definitely going to have to get a new leather waistcoat after this! Then he began to try and make plans for his escape at the end of this undignified journey.

But it was too late. The journey came to an end and Gerald was once more looking at a familiar black and red and white stitched boot. Gerald knew there was no hope now but tried not to show it. "Hallo Luther," he started but further witty comment was forced from his mind as he was hauled to his feet. Once more the sworn enemies stood face to face. Gerald knew that this time there was going to be no quick escape - but time would tell if this was to be a permanent state of affairs.

Luther looked at his latest catch with unconcealed glee. He gloated on his prize as he silently contemplated the pleasure that dealing with Gerald was going to give him. Finally he allowed himself a small, slight, smile. Gerald's blood ran cold. Luther saw the reaction and the smile became broader.

"Bring him," Luther barked, then turned and strode off down the corridors that led into the heart of his underground complex. The henchmen obeyed instantly and Gerald felt himself half carried, half hustled, after their boss. He knew the end would not now be long in coming.

Luther reached the door he had been marching towards. He unlocked it, using one of the large ring of keys he had taken from his belt. Throwing the door open he surveyed the scene that greeted him. This was his domain. This was his play room. Here he was going to have some fun. These thoughts of the pleasures to come were interrupted by the arrival of his henchmen and their Gerald baggage. Luther glared at them briefly before striding confidently into the room. He looked around, assessing what he saw with his practised eye. "I'm home," he thought to himself as he surveyed his lair.

The chamber that he looked into was roughly square. The marks on the walls showed that at some time it had been shaped by the hands of man – or dwarf. Much of the rock removed in this way had been used to form the wall that blocked what had once been a wider entrance. Now only the single sturdy door made of heavy oak beams set into a stout frame was the only way in or out. It was at this threshold that Luther stood, more or less central in one of the sides of the chamber.

On his immediate left, against the rough stone of the wall, stood a rack of shelves. Each shelf was laden with a row of jars and pots, no two alike in size or shape. Each jar contained a liquid of a hue drawn from one of the colours of the rainbow - and a few others. In most of the jars something floated. On one shelf the first jar contained a greenish liquid in which floated a hand. From the colour of the skin it probably originally belonged to a dark elf – except that it seemed to have 6 fingers. The liquid in the next jar had a yellow tinge. In this there were several ears. Some of them were clearly human, others obviously not. The largest seemed to be red in colour with tufts of purple hair sprouting from the pointed end. Further survey of this shelf revealed other jars, each of which contained different body parts. It was best not to look too closely at some of these jars for they contained things only usually seen in nightmares.

The next shelf was filled with skulls and jaw bones. Again it was easy to pick out the human ones amongst these. Others were simply too big or too long or of such a shape that it was clear they had come from something else. More nightmares awaited those who contemplated what that something else might be.

Another shelf was filled with more pots. Each bore a label to tell of its contents. Most of the labels could be read by anyone and the contents listed would have been familiar to a herbalist or an apothecary. These were mostly common ingredients for common purposes. On some of the others the writing was in more obscure script. While most of the alphabets would have been familiar to a sage they were impossible to read with a quick scan of the eyes. These must be the rarest ingredients that would only be used in small quantities in the most complex of recipes. As Luther looked this way from the doorway he knew this collection was the major part of his greatest treasure.

Against the wall opposite the door stood what was obviously a work bench. The surface of this bench was made of thick, rough sawn planks, worn white by their constant scrubbing. It stood four square on sections of tree trunk. It was clear that this is where the real work was done. A complex arrangement of glass flasks and tubing was assembled on this bench. It looked more like a three dimensional maze for a small rodent than anything having a practical purpose. However, on closer inspection, small drops of a golden coloured liquid that seemed to be glowing with an inner light was dripping from a spout at the heart of the glass tubes. Clearly something very special was being prepared by this construction.

Neatly stacked against the wall at the back edge stood more containers. Each was clearly labelled, all holding rare and unusual chemicals. Their arrangement spoke of the precision of the person who made use of them. Clearly everything was to hand, as were the tools on their rack alongside the bench. Some - like the saws and knives - had a clear purpose while others were destined for more exotic uses. I mean, what use did anyone have for a tea strainer with spikes around the rim on the end of a bendy piece of wire? The look in Luther's eyes as he inspected this bizarre equipment showed that he knew.

He was looking to his right now, along the length of that wall of the room. His gaze paused on what could only be a rack standing in the middle of the room. The bindings for wrists and ankles attached to the ropes passing over the rollers made that obvious. It was painted solid black. It had a shine that indicated that it had been recently washed to remove who knows what sort of stains. But it was not at this instrument of torture that the arch villain was directing his attention.

He was looking beyond the rack at the wall where, fastened firmly to a number of large iron rings were his captives. Tied by their wrists high above their heads his four earlier victims awaited his pleasure. Eldon was at one end. He had been stripped of his chain mail. Hanging there in his under tunic he had been totally deflated by the experience. No longer the young, energetic leader, he was now just another youth dressed in a simple shirt. Gertrude hung next to him. Somehow she still retained her detached air. Despite the ropes she still seemed to be in total control. Luther decided that this is where he would start – but not yet.

As he looked further along the line of prisoners Quickbeam came next. He still had the confused look about him as if he didn't understand what was happening. That was the same look that had led many a foe to underestimate his abilities. The way he had been stripped to his undergarments showed that Luther was not going to make that mistake. Lastly there was Thrugg. He had been tied with extra ropes because of his great strength. As Luther looked on he was testing them. Luther was pleased to see that they held. Thrugg, and the rest, would remain as his trophies. Luther would be able to do what he wanted with them in his own time.

This was the revelry that had been interrupted by the entrance of his hirelings half carrying the latest acquisition. Seeing Luther's raised hand his men stopped just outside the doorway. This had given Gerald a moment to look around in the room and see his restrained colleagues. Luther watched as he saw Gerald take in the situation. Luther's smile became a little wider as Gerald's shoulders sank even lower.

"Good," Luther thought, "Now all hope has gone." He knew that his victory was now complete. He turned to his men and ordered "Put him with the others." He had to contain his pleasure to avoid laughing out loud as he watched the henchmen dragging the compliant Gerald across the room to truss him up on one of the empty rings. Now the five brave adventurers hung side by side like chickens in a butcher's shop window - ready for the plucking. Or were they lambs ready for the slaughter?

Returning to their master, the men clustered behind Luther. They joined him in the admiration of the view. The pride in their triumph was plain to see in their body language. Hanging so that they were forced to stand on tiptoe, the adventurers could only look at the floor in their personal misery of defeat.

"Time to add a little tension to the situation," Luther thought to himself. With a toss of his head he indicated that everyone who could should leave. The thugs filed out, clearly happy with their achievement and looking forward to their reward. Luther, still wearing black gloves with their trademark red and white piping, picked up the lantern from the bench where it had been placed. He slowly walked along the line of prisoners. One by one he inspected them although none would meet his gaze. Finally, he turned and crossed to the door.

He paused, turned back and said: "Don't go away now. The party's about to begin." The door closed as he went out and the room was plunged into almost total darkness. The only light was coming from the stub of a single black candle burning in a saucer on the workbench.

The psychological tactic to deepen the despair seemed to be a success. The adventurers gave the impression of sinking deeper and deeper into their own thoughts. No one moved. They simply hung there, awaiting their fate.

Typically it was Gertrude who decided that something must be done. Raising her head she looked from one to another of her colleagues before directing a comment to them all: "Tell me again how we got into this mess." This drew a mixed reaction from those who hung alongside her.

Eldon looked sharply upwards and glared at her as if he was expecting her to blame him. Quickbeam seemed to be marshalling his thoughts, as if he was trying to divine some deeper truth from the simple request. Gerald simply hung there with his eyes closed, as if his defeat was complete. As many times before it fell to Thrugg to give an answer. Not the quickest of wits or sharpest of brains but often he was able to go to the heart of the matter. And his considered statements nearly always defined the truth of any situation. And this was the case now with his considered reply: "It was Rogo. He sent us."

Gertrude could have screamed with a mixture of frustration and relief. But instead she contented herself with a simple question: "Yes. But before that?" This time it was Quickbeam who had reached the end of his internal journey of contemplation: "It started with the kidnapping of that King ..." His voice trailed off as he, and all the other heroes, recalled the train of events that had ended with them hanging by their wrists awaiting an uncertain fate.

To be continued ...

Chapter 1: A Quiet Day in Sham

Imagine you are a bird, flying high over a wilderness landscape. You see below you that there are no signs of industry and very little of cultivation. You look down on mainly woods, heath lands, hills and mountains all criss-crossed with their fair share of rivers and streams. Everything looks peaceful in the noonday sunshine.

Now imagine that you possess the keen eyesight of a bird of prey. With this you can see more detail in the land below. Here is an isolated farmstead where some people are labouring in the fields. They seem to be gathering a harvest from the earth. From their bent backs it is some sort of root crop – potatoes probably. In the next field someone else is ploughing the ground with a team of oxen. They are making ready to sow seed again so that there will be another crop to harvest.

Next there is a large well built building surrounded by orchards. The nearby river has been dammed to produce a series of ponds. More fields surround the ponds and the building. These fields are enclosed by a fence. All within is well ordered and neat. All is tended by ant like men - and only men - clad in yellow and brown robes. Clearly an abbey or monastery or similar religious house.

With your inbuilt sense of direction you know that you are flying north. Something tells you that this is taking you towards the wilder regions of this land. Looking back, towards the south, in the far distance you can just make out the start of your journey. There are the signs of a town hard by mountains and a great lake. There are many large building at the heart of that settlement. The smaller dwelling places are crowded together around these. Largest and grandest is a castle like palace that has obviously been the centre of power for some time.

But your business was not there. You have left behind what passes for civilization in this realm and are heading towards the badlands.

How can you hope to find your way? How do you know where you are going in this seemingly trackless wilderness? You swoop lower, so as to get a closer look. And you see that the land is not trackless. You are following a dirt road through the woods, plains and hills. And it seems to be a busy road - or at least there are 3 or 4 groups of travellers making their way slowly along the muddy and rutted highway. It is never very wide. The route it takes tries to follow the flattest of the land. It snakes round the hills and threads a precarious way along the sides of the mountains that it passes through. The number of travellers and the well used appearance of this highway makes it clear that this is the principal route in this region.

Your instinct about the journey makes it clear that you are to follow this road. Continuing northwards you pass over a village. Perhaps it is a small town. There are certainly a greater number of cottages and larger houses clustered around the road. More have spilled outwards along minor routes leading to isolated farmsteads and mills set further away from the road. A market square stands at the heart of this settlement. This is probably where the main market for the region takes place for a small castle like structure dominates it. But the defences of this structure are not much to write home about.

It is little more than a simple tower with an inner and outer bailey for use of the locals in time of strife. In fact it is itself dominated by another, larger, edifice. This one seems to have the form and stature of a place of learning - a school or college perhaps. Maybe in this land a university even. The village town is a hive of activity with comings and goings and the local market is in full swing.

But your business is not here. Your journey continues northwards into the wilder and remoter regions that lie beyond this place. Well kept fields give way to rough scrublands. Hills covered with sheep become empty upland moors where wild beasts can be seen hunting for the scarce food. In places woods and forests crowd in on your road. There are no road wardens in this region to keep back the undergrowth and provide protection for the travellers. Now the road is quieter and the travellers fewer. Those who do journey seem to be cautious and favour small groups rather than larger caravans. No one rides, everyone walks and the road narrows and fades into the empty landscape.

In this emptiness the only buildings are a couple of inns on the road. They are sited on either side of a high pass where the road rises over the foothills of a mountain range crowding down on the thoroughfare. They have been built here to provide shelter for the traveller before the dangerous journey over this high pass is undertaken. The few scattered graves close to both of these inns show that this part of the journey is particularly dangerous.

Beyond the pass the land flattens out again. Again fertile fields fill this high plateau. Here a hard life can be lived out before the road once more meets mountains further north. But as you cross this landscape something else comes into view. And now you feel the journey is almost over. Amidst the hills and forests of this wild region someone is building another castle. This is a far grander affair than the one in the middle of the university village town. Or, at least, it will be one day.

It is surrounded by a high curtain wall standing more than the height of 5 men. There is a round tower at each corner rising half as high again. While it is clear from the scaffolding and piles of stones that it is still being built, the castle is already more than half finished. At its heart stands the central keep. The walls of this are complete.

Guards are posted by the main gateway. They control who has access to the interior of this building where the kitchens, halls, bed chambers, dungeons and cellars can be found. There is very little movement in or out of this building. The courtyard in front however remains a hive of activity. The insect like workmen dress and trim stones for the rest of the construction that goes on at a pace around them.

You know that you have arrived. This is surely your destination. But why is a castle being built here? There seems to be no threat from the farmsteads that share the plateau. There are no other large constructions in the region that this castle might challenge. It seems totally out of place.

You start to circle to get your bearings - to see what sort of place this is. And then you see the other road. This one runs east to west and meets the south to north line of your journey just south west of the castle to be. Both look equally well travelled. This is certainly an important cross roads for nearby are two bridges - one on each road. The one on the north-south road is stone built. It has been here for a very long time. Clearly time has worked on it for there are signs that it has been recently repaired.

The east-west road has a wooden bridge. This is also of sturdy construction but seems newer - almost as if it has been completed within the last couple of months. Looking closer you can see the remains of earlier structures scattered along the sides of the young river that they both cross. Clearly wood is not as durable as stone in this foothill region.

The river is full of energy. Beyond these crossing points, as you look to the north, you see the mountain range that has given it birth. This is no small obstacle to further travel, although the road you have followed this far continues onwards and upwards towards the heights. As the mountains close in you can just discern the high pass amid the clouds that it needs to cross their mass. As you look to the west and to the north you realise that you are looking into an empty land in both directions. You have obviously reached the very edge of civilization.

So, that explains the castle. This is a border point on the two routes. He who controls the castle will control the roads - and the land beyond to the south and east. The bridges would be key defensive positions should anyone try to enter the fertile heartland you have flown over from the badlands beyond. And yet the castle is unfinished. Work continues at an urgent pace and you sense that what you seek is not to be found amongst the dust and toil. A closer look around is needed and you swoop lower.

The castle is not alone. Nearby there is a scattering of buildings - as if bits have dropped off in the construction of the fortress. Close by the north-south road, just beyond the bridge and hard against the woods stands an isolated cottage. It hurts your eyes to look at it. It seems to be changing shape. Shadows are forever moving over its surface. You can sense even at a distance that great power is contained within that simple structure and it is struggling to contain it. Even the garden close to it is weird. Paths and low hedges have been laid out in intertwining geometric patterns. At their heart sits a single man clad in brown flowing robes. He is waiting for something. As you watch, a creature - a goblin perhaps - emerges from the pulsating house carrying a tray. There is something on the tray. The servant, for it is obvious that is what the creature is, threads its way by a complicated route around the network of pathways towards the brown clad human. As the journey ends the man takes the drinking vessel - for that is now clearly what it is. He raises it to his lips and drinks. The pathways seem to re-arrange themselves into a fresh design and the cottage once more twists and turns as it changes its outward appearance under some powerful external influences.

Only the foolish would visit that cottage.

To the north and west, hard by the crossroads, stands a tall tower. It appears to be carved out of a single enormous block of ebony. It is solid black in colour, shimmering under the sunlight. This is obviously a residence worthy of a mystic or mage of great power. As you watch smoke suddenly billows out of a window, unseen until this moment, about halfway up the tower. Another creature's head - again probably a goblin - appears from behind the smoke. He is obviously in some discomfort. Suddenly he is flying through the air - downwards. Now in the window stands a human. He is clad in clothes that match the tower. Black robes mark him as the owner and the powerful mage you'd expect to meet within. He is obviously not pleased with the goblin and has decided to teach him a lesson.

The goblin, screaming in terror, is travelling quite fast now towards a sticky end. Suddenly the mage makes a gesture and the goblin is silenced in mid scream. Motionless, apart from the movement generated by the force of gravity, the goblin continues in his downwards journey. He lands with a sickening thump. A few seconds later he suddenly sits bolt upright. He leaps to his feet, brushes himself down and disappears around the back of the tower. You realise you have seen a master disciplining an apprentice for making a mistake. This is obviously not a place to visit either.

Between the two magical residences, and closer to the crossroads, there is a mismatched collection of hovels and cottages. These are obviously where the real people live. It is to these you are drawn. You sweep lower to land on the east-west road to the east of the crossroads. Settling in the street - if you could call the short section of dirt road covered with broken stones a street - you look around yourself. Most of these wattle and daub buildings are clearly the homes of the residents of this isolated community. While they have the same basic construction, the personal touches of flowers in hanging baskets and roses around the doors make each one unique. There are the buildings that people call "home". However, one or two stand out as different.

Standing hard by the castle is another building. This one is older for the stonework shows clearly the passage of time. Even though it has been decorated in a variety of styles, it is clearly a temple or religious house. Maybe the diversity in the decoration speaks of the different allegiances amongst those who worship within its walls but there seems to be no conflict. The few you can see coming and going through its high and wide main entrance greet one another as friends as they pass. It stands in well kept and ordered grounds tended by gardeners. It is as if those who oversee this place impose an order on all users - ensuring a vital facility is maintained for the good of all. While this building is impressive, its very order seems to deny any hope of interest for the casual visitor within. Your eye is taken by another construction which looks much more intriguing.

Nearer the crossroads, on the other side of the street, is a wooden building that has a much more slapdash style. The main body of this building faces the road. It is obviously as old as the temple but of a more practical - rather than spiritual - design. Wings have been added to each end of the original building, running away from the road. Obviously there is some sort of inner courtyard contained by these. To one side there is a series of small, rude shacks. Each one seems to contain a secret of its own. The main roof is low and few windows pierce the front wall. The narrow doorway makes it clear that this place has a more secretive purpose. And yet people are cheerfully passing freely in and out. It is certainly busier than the temple opposite and seems to serve a more important purpose in this village.

You know that this is where you should go. You feel that here the story will begin. You sense that in this place the events that will unfold will affect the destinies of many different people. This is where you have to go and watch what happens.

As you move closer and become one of the crowd - if 30 people can be a crowd - you can see that the object of your attention is an inn. For all its age and air of mystery it is nothing more than a simple wayside tavern. In the wind the sign hanging above the doorway swings from side to side. The picture on it is of a jovial, winged, creature holding a smoking pipe. Alongside where he sits there is an over flowing drinking horn. He needs to watch his weight. He wears a green waistcoat and a blue hat and seems to be enjoying himself. The words on the sign confirm your first observation. This is "The Portly Pixie".

But there is still something missing. Amongst the crowd who are gathering, clearly expecting something to happen, no one stands out. They are the simple village folk that you would find almost anywhere at the edge of civilization. Farmers marked by their work clothes have come fresh from the fields. Young boys squabble and chatter amongst their elders as street urchins do everywhere that crowds gather. One or two barflies, clearly worse for wear, lean against the horse trough outside the tavern as if contemplating drowning themselves in the murky water in an attempt to get rid of their hangovers. Beggars move up and down the street, haranguing the crowds with pleas for alms. Off to one side, towards the temple, stands a small group. Their clothes mark them as members of some religious order. You realise that earlier you saw similar yellow and brown clothed people working in the monastery's fields.

All in all it looks like ordinary people lining an ordinary street amid an extraordinary landscape. It shouldn't be like this. Where are the adventurers of whom the tales will be told? Where are the mighty warriors who will carry the day? Where are the ones who will rescue the princess or save the world? Where are the heroes of whom the bards will one day sing?

Then it comes to you. Like anyone with any sense, they're out of the noon day sun enjoying a quiet liquid lunch before the rigours of an afternoon sleeping it off. Inside the low doorway is where we will find our cast of characters. And it is in that half light that the real story begins:

Rogo the inn keeper is stood behind the serving table. He had just finished taking the clean tankards out of the not so clean water he had been washing them in. He had dried them one by one on a cloth that got grimmer by the wipe. "Still, it will improve the flavour of the ale," he thought to himself using the same cloth to wipe the table top. Musing further, he made a mental note to get Megan to change the washing water before the evening rush - if you could call 7 people a rush.

Then he remembered, almost in terror, that today was Friday. Friday was the end of the working week. And Friday was when Markenbrat paid his masons and labourers at the castle. And those masons and labourers were all dwarves. And those dwarves only knew one thing to do with their money.

"Stumpy!" he shouted. From out the back, through the kitchen door, emerged a stooped shape. It shuffled a little as if walking was difficult. It wore an off-white apron and a chequered piece of cloth was wound round the strangely misshapen head. This was obviously the cook but looked like no other cook ever seen in a respectable kitchen. But, after all, what did you expect? Stumpy was not human. With his thick, wart covered, brown skin and pig nose he was almost a perfect example of an orc, for orc he was

As well as cook, he was also Rogo's current stand in bar boy while Bert rested his back again. "Bring up another three barrels of the heavy ale when you get a chance," Rogo instructed him. With a nod of the head the orc headed out back again to resume duties in the kitchen. Lunch today was going to be interesting, as it always was when Zama took a day off.

At the far end of the bar table a head suddenly rose and vacant eyes stared desperately around the room. Almost human, except for the slightly pointed nose and the trace of whiskers, you could tell that something had suddenly woken this customer out of a deep sleep. Rogo reflected that Skutlar the skaven had been resting at that end of the bar table since about three hours after sunset on the previous evening. "At least he's still alive," Rogo thought to himself, "though with Skutlar it was often hard to tell." If further proof was needed it came as the figure croaked a single word: "Ale." Rogo then realised what had awoken this customer - his mention of heavy ale to Stumpy - and acknowledged the reincarnation with a friendly nod. He moved along the table and placed a freshly dried, mostly clean, tankard before the current holder of the meaningless office of Mayor.

Once more Skutlar barked the single word as if it was an order, although it came out more as a croak from his dehydrated throat. "Ale". Rogo reached behind him for the serving jug and poured a generous measure for his friend. After all, he had been a good customer last night - and the night before that - and the night before that! In fact he was currently the inn's second best customer with only Mandrake regularly out drinking him. Skutlar groped for the tankard with half closed eyes and sank the contents in a single swallow. As the ale entered his system a change seemed to come over the Mayor. Life seemed to return to the half dead drinker.

Skutlar sat up and began to take stock of his surroundings. He noticed, while trying not to look too closely at it, that the daylight was trying to penetrate the gloom of the tavern's interior. He searched the shadows vainly for his fellow drinkers of the previous evening. Finding none he was forced to the inevitable conclusion. "It's Friday?" he asked Rogo. Rogo confirmed the conclusion with another nod of the head as he refilled the empty tankard. Returning the nod to mark his thanks, Skutlar began the emptying process again. This time he drank more slowly, savouring each sip. Even with his jaded taste buds he knew that Rogo had served him the best ale.

Rogo waited patiently and with some amusement for the inevitable. The update on the day of the week slowly worked it's way into the skaven's brain and had an immediate effect. Rogo saw it happen. Suddenly Skultar stopped dead. You could sense the cogs turning. Friday - Markenbrat - Dwarves - Pay day - Heavy ale - A good drinking night! The smile began to spread over the face of the tavern's only conscious customer. He was looking forward to a good evening.

17

In his newly found jovial mood Skutlar's thoughts moved on. There were more pressing and important matters that now required the attention of the town's principal representative. Much more urgent than drinking all day. "Will lunch be long?" he asked Rogo. The innkeeper considered his reply carefully. He had seen Stumpy struggling with "lunch" earlier. It took some effort even for the orc to get the snake into the kitchen - it was that large. And while he knew the overall length of the reptile, Rogo had no idea how much of it his chef du jour would put in each bun. Before he could frame a reply Skutlar moved on: "Never mind. Give me another while I wait" came the instruction.

Rogo lifted another jug - not the best ale this time he thought - and topped up the half empty tankard. Skutlar greeted him with his next question: "Was it because of the dwarves?" Rogo looked at him wondering what the dwarves had to do with the length of the lunch. Skutlar rambled on, saving Rogo the problem of sorting that out: "You know. Why you built the inn here. Because you'd get the trade from that pile of stone that one day will become a castle?"

Rogo considered the question. He let his mind drift back over the 16 - no 17 - years since he and his friends had come to the region known as Sham. He remembered it as if it was yesterday. And in his mind he returned to that former arrival time. He recalled the story that he regularly told about the founding of the village and the naming of the inn.

Chapter 2: The Meeting at the Crossroads

The wind had been whistling in from the east that day, and into the faces of the small group of travellers. It had brought with it a little snow and an awful lot of dust. Rogo was once more thinking about the cloaked figures paused at the cross-roads strangely set in the middle of nowhere. He remembered one of the more warlike members of the group muttering under his breath, but in a voice just loud enough to be heard by those closest to him, "Bloody fine place to build a castle!"

That's when Rogo had looked at Zama with a strange twinkling in his eye and the usual quirk on his lips. "Bloody fine place seems to say it all," he said. Zama laughed quietly to herself in the way that won many a heart. "I know what you mean," she replied, "and it seems so far from what we knew." Then it was Rogo's turn to laugh. Throwing back his hood he had looked about him, surveying what was to be the newest base for their sometime shady operations. "So far..." he echoed as his mind cast back over the miles, every long one of them, and the hours that had been passed while this strange collection of independent spirits had made their journey from what was to what was to be.

It had been a long trek to these badlands. It had all started earlier when they had been hauled before the Duke, seated on his golden throne. Well, that was what most people saw but to the expert eyes of Rogo and Zama standing motionless before him it looked more like plaster gilt. And to think it was once solid gold! For the present the Duke was not pleased, and that was an understatement.

"I can't prove it," he had said with some force, "I have no physical evidence, but if I could you two would be listening to me stretched out on the racks in the deepest of my torture chambers. I know - as you do - that someone has upset the High Priest. I know - as you do - that someone disrupted the Grand Conclave of the Disciples of Kalaar that was being held at the Temple - although where they got the stinkbats from I'll never know! And I know - as you do - that everyone tells me it was you two who were behind it. But I can't prove it."

That's when Rogo and Zama had exchanged glances that seemed to say that this was another small victory in their campaign to bring excitement into the settled lives around them. Unfortunately, that look hadn't gone unnoticed and the Duke snapped: "Will you two at least try and look penitent when I'm telling you off! This can't go on. You're making my life a misery. I spend more time fielding the complaints about the activity of you and your so-called Adventurers Club than I do running all the rest of my Dukedom. It has got to stop."

"But, sire, ..." Zama started.

"Not another word!" came the interruption. "I know you what you're up to. That silver tongue of yours ties my mind in knots and I don't know if I'm coming or going. It's time you went off again. That's the only answer. You did me good service in quelling the rebellion in Derfsgape - even if you did ruin the City in the process - and that's why I've given you your heads up to now. But the holiday's over. You want to live as nobility? Well then, you're going to have to earn it.

"I'm sending you north and west, to the border lands. My agents have told me that things are getting out of their control and a show of strength is needed. I'm organising a party to go there and build a castle for me. Some of them are going of their own free will. Some are bound by honour to go. Some of them have no choice - I've bound them in iron chains.

"Make your own choices - you and those ..." he groped for a word worthy of Ducal lips, "... miscreants! Go with honour at your own free wills. Or go some other way. You two, if you choose, can be in charge. You can control them, use them, exploit them for a change. Make their lives a misery instead of mine. Maybe by the time the castle's finished, things will have cooled down enough for you to come back - but don't count on it. Plan on staying there. Build a village or something.

"Now - do you go freely, or do I have you taken?"

Rogo had remembered that conversation as he waited at the rendezvous. Yes, it had been a long road to reach this windswept spot with those gathered about him at the cross-roads. There was Karak Ominar, who had earlier commented on the suitability of the chosen location. All spit and polish, chain mail and helmet. Clearly a captain of the Duke's militia. He was chief escort - or should that be jailer? - to the party and led the squad of men at arms chosen to garrison the area.

Next to him stood a dwarf. From the condition of his battleaxe and the armour that he wore, this was no ordinary dwarf. He stood with his red hair blowing free in the cold wind. He showed no sign of any discomfort even though he had recently removed his chain mail. Bare-chested he was defying the cold east wind. And the east wind seemed to be avoiding him. No body or no thing messed with Markenbrat, the dwarf lord. It was he who had brought the masons and labourers to see to the building of the new border fortress.

Then there were the other displaced members of the Adventurer's Club - and a motley crew they were! All of them were wrapped in their cloaks against the bitter wind but each of them had their own individual character. Rogo could see them now.

First there was Mandrake. Even to a casual observer it was clear that this was a user of magic. The brown robes with their flowing sleeves spoke to his craft as did the small book that was never out of his hand. He seemed bemused as he looked around. Another city dweller thrust unwillingly into the middle of the wild country. But appearances can be deceptive, particularly in Mandrake's case. It was only when you got to know him better that you realised just how powerful this mage was.

The first thing most people noticed about him was that he never quite looked the same. Rogo could even remember times when he had turned into a she for a few days. All this was brought about by his intense interest in shapes and their relevance to the world about. He investigated their power with a passion and channelled the knowledge gained into working magic with style. Yes, Mandrake was a great wizard - if only he could focus his attention on the matter in hand and get his eyes off the next jug of honey mead!

The next brown robed figure was Meglos. His robes were different in their cut and spoke of the religious nature of his leanings. Looking every inch the monk clad in simple homespun robes you could have mistaken him for having a peaceful nature if it wasn't for the large two-handed sword he leant on. This was Resolution, badge of office of the Highest Priest in the church of Yorkus, the god of war - and other things. It was good to have him on your side and Rogo knew his skills were going to be needed in the taming of these lands.

The next figure wore black. Despite the snow still being driven onto them by the wind, his clothes refused to give up their obscurity. This was Nyazam, skilled in all those martial forms associated with his craft. It was said that one such as he could pass through a crowded market square in daylight and never be seen. If he chose he could enter the most closely guarded bed chamber at the dead of night to emerge with that held most dear by the one who slept therein. He was not an assassin because he had no interest in money. His skills were given freely to those who he respected as his equal or better. Rogo remembered being glad that Nyazam was on Rogo's team.

The rest of this bedraggled group were the foot soldiers - Targon, Naructer, Kloram Kyol, Zed, and Mudge - all so useful in those desperate times of the Derfsgape rebellion. None of them looked out of the ordinary but each brought to the group an essential specialist skill as well as innate combat ability and unquestioning loyalty to their friends.

And then there was Gerald. The only one of the Adventurer's Club who saw no real reason to leave the bright lights and flesh pots of the Capital. There were much richer pickings there than could ever be found in these borderlands. Gerald found out the hard way that the Duke meant what he said. Even now he stood with chains about his wrists and ankles, held firmly on either side by a pair of the biggest of Markenbrat's dwarves. As Rogo remembered his friend at those cross-roads, he remembered that it was only Gerald's friendship for Rogo that had prevented him disappearing several times on the long journey northwards. Chains could never hold him but loyalty could. Rogo had mused to himself "Must do something about those chains now," as he looked at his friend. And soon after they were struck off, Gerald became a full member of the exiles.

Then Zama had said "Here they come", breaking into the silence. Indeed through the dust filled, snow flecked, wind three dim figures could be seen approaching, with the faint sound of music coming before them,

"Who is it that we're meeting?" Karak had asked grumpily. "The Duke's local advisers," Zama answered him for the umpteenth time, "Springfever the golem maker, Fernlace the Druid, and the one they call The Piper." "Maker of music, worker of wonders, friend of all," Rogo had said, completing the litany.

To all of that Markenbrat had muttered with his usual dwarven directness, "Right load of weirdos".

And for once he was right. The newcomers had seemed more than a little weird as they approached the dust clad caravan. Perhaps strangest of all was the way they seemed untouched by the wind - as if the Piper's music was holding at bay the chilling blast. It was this aura of warmth and stillness that soon enfolded the waiting throng. It was a good beginning to the new age.

Later that same evening, as they sat by the side of their campfire relaxing after their meal, Rogo and Zama reflected on how smoothly everything had gone. Their badges of authority had been accepted and agreement quickly reached on how best to integrate this latest of the Duke's commands into the local harmony overseen by his agents. Even Fernlace had agreed on the chosen site when he saw no trees would have to die to allow the castle's building. He was even looking forward to the building of the new village and the joys it would bring.

Zama had come to a decision. "We shall call the village Sham," she announced. "Good idea," agreed Rogo, with very little thought, "and do you know what Fernlace said to me? He hoped there would be a good inn in this village." "Now, there's an idea," the fellow conspirator mused. "All we need now is a name."

"Do you remember Falstaff, that overweight pixie we met in Derfsgape...?"

Chapter 3: Drinking Disturbed

Smiling to himself in the remembrance of the warmth of those times, Rogo was reluctant to return to the present. But he did and, with a sigh brought his attention back to the 17 years later, Friday lunchtime. Then he replied to Skutlar's question. "No," he said simply, "It wasn't because of the dwarves." The tavern returned to its pre-luncheon calm.

All of a sudden the door to the street burst open. A woman standing taller than most men, with a slim build that spoke of great energy held within her frame and clothed in grey robes strode into the body of the inn. "That's it, I've had enough. I'm not waiting any longer," she threw over her shoulder at the dapper young man who trailed after her. At first glance you could tell that her pursuer was a warrior because of the armour he wore. You could also tell that he spent more time polishing it than making use of it for even in the dim light of the inn it sparkled and shone. A wise man would say he had gained it from inherited money rather than experience. But a wise man would also look at the weapons the bore and realise that this was no man to be trifled with.

He seemed to be losing the current battle though. He was trying to stop the woman he was following by the force of his words alone: "But, Gertrude ..." he prodded at her. But he might have tried to stop an elephant with a toothpick. Furious the priest, for that is what she clearly was, turned on her tormentor: "Eldon. Understand me. It's hot. It's dusty. There are lots of people out there. And he's not even the king of Chouse!" She hammered each point home with a jab of her forefinger into the chest of the man. Each blow seem to deflate him a little more, much to the amusement of the small crowd which had drifted in from the street to follow the action.

Eldon gave up and sat at the nearest table in the inn. The small crowd, now obviously his companions, joined him. There was a man mountain who had to stoop to get in the door. He was clearly a warrior for every muscle rippled and glistened on his body. Weapons that would have taken at least a couple of normal men to wield dangled like playthings on his belt. This was Thrugg, one of the strongest to live in the region of Sham.

Next to enter was one clad in mage's robes that sparkled and shone with his power. When you looked at his face you saw a man of more mature years. In a mage that spoke of danger for with age came experience and with experience came power. This was Quickbeam, the gentle mage. As if to prove it he even placed a hand on Eldon's shoulder to offer him a measure of support and comfort. This was swiftly shaken away, clearly in a fit of pique. This produced smiles among the current residents of the inn - except Eldon that is. Having made her points and got her way as usual, Gerturde turned to Rogo.

"How long will lunch be, Rogo?" she asked. Rogo thought to himself "What is it with these people? Why can't they just settle for the piece of the snake that's put in their bun? What difference does its length make?" Out loud he replied: "I'll just go and ask Stumpy" and turned for the kitchen door. He was halted in this act by Gertrude's cutting voice of authority: "Hold it!" Without thinking Rogo stopped dead in his tracks. He wanted to ask Gertrude if she'd learnt that tone of voice from Zama but before he could frame the question Gertrude went on:

"You mean, Stumpy's making lunch?" "Yes," Rogo replied, "It's Friday." He knew that was sufficient explanation for most people. "Just bread and cheese then," Gertrude decided, "And a fruit juice." She left the centre of the tavern to sit with her companions at the table where Eldon had all but collapsed.

Eldon looked quickly around his table, catching the eyes of his other companions. He shouted across the inn: "Make that 5 lots of bread and cheese and our usuals, please, Rogo." Rogo waved his acknowledgement and began pouring the drinks.

A short time later he was watching Skutlar heartily tucking into a double portion of Stumpy's snake in a bun. Rogo was disgusted. He got himself some bread, a little cheese and a small measure of his special reserve to add to the order and moved towards Eldon's table. He hoped to make conversation - and perhaps a little profit - with some of his other best customers. As he approached them, he considered what he knew about each of them.

Well, his old friend Gerald had brought them together. And there he sat at their heart quietly in the half light of the tavern. He was doing his favourite trick of fading into the background. The not quite black clothes he always wore helped but it was the way he sat that made the eye skid over him. So still, so not there, so much part of whatever it was he sat on or leaned against. Rogo had seen him stand in the middle of the street outside The Portly Pixie one summer's afternoon and be ignored by everyone walking up and down. That was until the dog started sniffing at him, thinking he was a hitching post or some other territory marker.

Over the years Rogo had seen Gerald do many things. Rogo had lost count of the times the broken bridge on the old capital road had been sold to newcomers! He'd even managed to sell the franchise on that con onto Wulf Godslayer! Still, Gerald was generous with his kickbacks and always chose the times when Zama wasn't around. People had to learn, didn't they? And it was only money. Then there were the extra pieces of treasure that seemed to appear from nowhere when his friends had finished trading their collected goods. You could count on Gerald to bring the small, exquisite and reasonably valuable piece of silverware.

And it's not as if the rest of them didn't know what was going on. In their early days together Rogo had watched fascinated as the returning adventurers had strip searched Gerald as they returned to the inn following an expedition. And he still had two small silver goblets to trade in as his personal treasure! No, Eldon, Gertrude and the rest had given up trying to find where he hid things a long time ago. They seemed to accept that Gerald earned his bonus.

Rogo looked at his friend - even though it took some effort to see the details. With one foot resting on the knee of the other leg Rogo could tell with his practised eye that even here Gerald was ready for action. The right hand resting on the raised leg just happened to be right alongside one of the boot daggers he always carried.

It was clear that Gerald was listening to the casual conversation happening around the table - he joined in with the occasion bursts of laughter. But his eyes were never still. He watched everyone and no-one. And whenever the door to the inn opened Gerald always knew who had come and gone. He sat facing the front door, while being able to keep his eye on the kitchen door as well. It was clear that the rest of the group trusted him with these duties and acknowledged that he was their scout.

Rogo's practised eye took in the clothing that Gerald favoured as his working gear. As an experienced scout - well he was still alive, wasn't he? - Gerald knew that shadows and night were never pure black. To blend in you had to dress to match the shades of darkness found in those places. No weapons were visible but Rogo knew that Gerald never carried fewer than 4 daggers. Using his experience, Rogo could have probably detected them in no time but this was his friend. Even in Sham you had to trust some people else you'd never get anywhere.

And Gerald had settled on the rest of the group now sitting around the table as the people he had chosen to trust. He had spoken to Rogo at length about the strengths amongst this group of brave adventurers. Over the years they had shown their ability to work as an efficient and successful team. Rogo may have had his doubts when Gerald first told him who he was hitching up with but time had told. It had been profitable for all.

As Rogo got closer to the table he considered the others who sat with Gerald. The leader of the group was clearly Eldon - to the uneducated eye, that is. Seated in the central position he seemed to dominate the table and steer the conversation. It was he who gave the orders based on the consensus of his colleagues' opinions. Luckily the rest of the group trusted him.

When Eldon had first arrived in Sham he knew little of the ways of the world. He was the third son of a minor noble with a small fortified manor house just off the Battenburgh road. Having no land to inherit and not fancying the Duke's standing militia, he had chosen to enter a church. Eldon became a lay brother at the nearby Trotslow Abbey at the age of 15. There he was able to learn the hard way about all the gods before deciding which one he would personally serve. The monks at Trotslow had a simple system of education.

Seekers after knowledge were given boring and mundane tasks to perform. Often these were also unpleasant. If they complained, it was explained that being subservient in life made it easier to be subservient to a god. If they bridled at this work, they were told that was exactly what was intended – to teach self reliance and promote energetic endeavour, before being soundly beaten and sent back to cleaning out the latrines.

In the end, as a result of the frustration born out of the meaningless and unexplained tasks, the acolytes nearly always ended up by calling upon a god for help. In this way their personal deity was selected.

After three years of suffering servitude (not quite the longest that acolyte training had been endured) Eldon had settled on Logos, truth, and following the advice of Father Michael, the Abbott, had left the Abbey for a time to experience the evils of the real world. The dishevelled and half naked state in which he arrived in Sham two days later testified to his success in that objective. Rogo's nose wrinkled even now remembering the smell of ditch water.

But now an altogether different Eldon sat at the head of this particular table. The chain mail shirt he wore shone from the daily polishing he made sure it received. The tabard with the coat of arms of his family had been hand stitched by an a elf maid who had a misplaced crush on him. However, it was elven workmanship and it had stood the test of time, adventure and the various other indignities visited upon it. Rogo wondered if Eldon would ever learn to read the script that the elf had used to write the motto below the crest. He might then have a different feeling about being seen out in it in mixed company.

But as with many things, Eldon didn't do what he could get others to do for him. His job was to make the difficult decisions of the leader. And those who could read what was written on his chest, shared the joke privately. None of them wanted to undermine Eldon's confidence or question his right to lead. Yes, he was seen as the natural leader - loud, direct, decisive, confident - and just a little bit stupid.

Gertrude was the power behind Eldon. Sitting quietly in her off-white robes she looked every inch the priest. Eyes hidden by the cowl that was always up seemed to be downcast as befitted her status. But Rogo knew they too missed nothing that went on around her. The hands meekly in her lap were never far away from weapons and spell book.

As had been seen in the earlier exchanges she had the common sense. That suited her calling as healer. Gerald had courted her well. She knew that Eldon had to do what she wanted - and that she had to keep at least one eye on Gerald at all times. As a follower of The One True God she knew there was good and bad in the world, along with those who lived in the cracks. As a disciple of Zama's she knew how to swing a mace to make sure that the world saw things her way!

Many an orc and ogre had misjudged her outwardly clerical appearance and gone to meet their god with a sore head. Yes, Gertrude was out to rid the world of all disharmony and wasn't scared to get rid of those who were causing it as part of her master plan.

Thrugg was altogether another type of adventurer. Seated at the table he was taller than most of the other tavern customers standing up. The well muscled body was clad in workmanlike leather armour - well oiled to give maximum flexibility, well marked to show it's necessity.

The immense two handed sword that was laid on the table before him declared his trade. He was a fighter. Pure and simple - a fighter. He was pure because he didn't know any different. And he wasn't that simple. You just have to be careful how you say things to Thrugg.

Rogo smiled to himself as he remembered the story Gerald told him after one of this band's forays. They had been exploring this complex of caves and chambers to recover some missing treasure. "Well, someone had had to lose it for it turn up there, didn't they?" is how Gerald had put it. Standing in a large chamber they had been faced with a choice of ways forward. Eldon had ordered Thrugg to guard one of the two doors. Only he hadn't quite said it that way.

"Thrugg, the door," is what Eldon had barked. Thrugg duly strode over to the door. He paused as he assessed its strength and decided it was not that strong. Eldon watched bemused as his designated guard crouched a little. Next the fingers were forced under the quite large gag at the bottom. Thrugg was clearly straining then as he used the considerable power in his legs to lift the heavy oak door. It was not long before he had pulled it completely off its hinges. Rising he took a fresh grip on the sides, lifted it easily and brought it across the room to Eldon.

Unfortunately Eldon and Thrugg's fellow adventurers were not the only ones who had noticed the removal of the door from its appointed place. In the room beyond, revealed by the sudden removal of the door, there were at least 20 orcs. At first they were frozen into immobility by the disappearance of the wooden slab that kept the wind out. Everyone knew that this situation was not going to last long. It was Eldon who reacted first amongst the treasure seekers. Unfortunately he started to panic and made things worse:

"Thrugg, look behind the door! Quick!" he bleated out in desperation. Instead of looking into the room he had exposed Thrugg, ponderously peered around the door he still held, coming nose to face with Eldon. "Yes, Eldon?" he politely enquired. "Not this way, over there" came the even more panicky reply accompanied by much pointing into the room with the now wide open doorway.

In the room the orcs were beginning to recover. They had put down the beer flagons from which they had been drinking and the hunks of meat they were eating and were arming themselves. It was clear that they were making moves towards what they hoped would be the fresh human meat of a post dinner snack. Eldon was gripped with panic now. His mouth had become totally disconnected from his brain. All he could manage to say was "Thrugg ... Thrugg .... Thrugg ..." His one hard man strike force was still standing facing him around the edge of the door he still held, patiently waiting for further instructions.

Gerald had told Rogo he was having great difficulties in hiding in the nearby shadows because he was laughing so much. Even though death faced them all the situation was so bizarre that you had to laugh. However, the scout knew someone was going to have to do something before it was too late. As usual it was Gertrude who saved the day. "Thrugg," she barked, "Take the door and hit the orcs with it until they stop moving." The requested action took almost less time than the request had taken to be made. Once more Thrugg had saved the day - or had it been Gertrude?

Yes, you could count on Thrugg the fighter to do what you asked him to - to do exactly what you asked him to.

And that left Quickbeam. It almost hurt the eye to look too long at him. His robes seemed to have a life of their own and often changed colour to match their wearer's mood. Woe betides the enemy that saw those robes flash red and white!

Their cut - with all the fullness and wide sleeves to hide the concealed pockets within them - proclaimed his trade to all. A mage from the Mandrake school of stylish magic. Highly skilled at making the honey mead disappear but with more common sense than the Guild's leader - or a greater capacity for his drink.

Gerald knew the team had to have someone who openly could be seen to be the brains of the outfit if he was going to get away with things without detection. He had waited a long time to add Quickbeam to their group. Mages come and go quite often in the backwater of Sham. Except Memnon that is. He's still hanging around long after he's dead. But that is a story involving the dangers of opening unlocked chests and releasing flying swords while hiding from another threat to life and for another time.

Quickbeam was different from the first. Having first studied the element of fire, he had the speed of thought and quickness of eye necessary to survive in the borderlands. Moving on to follow the mysteries of the magic of the mind under the elf Glows himself had made him doubly useful in the quest. And he was not interested in material things - only in expanding his collection of magical bits and bobs. Just the right person for Gerald who much preferred to come back with the bright, shiny, things that Rogo turned into hard cash.

Yes, the team of adventurers sat round the table were probably Sham's finest of the moment - which meant they were unlikely to be welcomed anywhere else in Chouse! Just what Rogo and Zama needed to keep the informal sort of law and order they practised in the region. Their code wasn't an eye for an eye. It was more an arm and a leg along with whatever it was you took in the first place. The Duke had required organisation of them - he had left the means up to them.

And, for the present, Rogo was happy to wait upon the table of the most efficient of the current means employed in that mission.

As Rogo set down the food and drinks he couldn't help overhearing the conversation. Thrugg was saying "And then we met that talking dog..." They were clearly re-living the events of the time Zama sent them to look for Idaho Smith the naturist - no naturalist Rogo reminded himself for the umpteenth time. What a lark that had been! It had nearly got them all killed!

"It was 'The Entertainer'," Eldon told Thrugg. There was a pause. Rogo watched closely to see if he could see the cogs turning inside the muscled fighter's head. But there was no perceptible movement as Thrugg digested what he had been told. Finally a conclusion surfaced.

"No, it was definitely a talking dog," Thrugg concluded, "and not at all entertaining." Rogo perched on the edge of a nearby table and set his tray down alongside him. "This is going to be worth listening to," he thought to himself, "and probably quite funny." Thrugg's considered reply didn't end with the simple statement. He was going on to give a concise account of his recollections of that particular quest:

"Zama used her special powers to send us as close as she could to where Idaho was. We ended up in that cave, huddled together on that narrow ledge. In the end Gertrude had the sense to get the lantern out of your haversack because you were scared to let go of the rocks you were holding to stop you falling off. You were scared of the dark." This was too much for Eldon who tried to interrupt: "I was not scared ..." he started.

Thrugg raised a restraining hand the size of a dinner plate. "Let me finish, Eldon," he said, politely but firmly. Gerald decided to join in: "You've always told me that it is rude to interrupt a good story," he said. The twinkle in his eyes and the jingle in his voice told Rogo that Gerald was sharing the fun. Eldon simply shut up and fumed - glaring at no-one and everyone.

Thrugg, impervious to the events around him, took up his narrative once more: "As I was saying, Gertrude got the lantern and as soon as we could see I led the way into the next cave. There was this giant frog which spat poison at me. I hit him and it didn't spit any more. Quickbeam had to use his magic to deal with the frog's lizard men pets." Quickbeam acknowledged his masterly role with a single nod of the head as Thrugg continued:

"Then Gertrude put me back together and we all went into their sleeping place. That's where we found all those rare shells. Next we worked our way further along the rocky ledge at the side of the pool and found the writing on the wall. Once we'd overcome the puzzle, we got the temple door open and in the antechamber after the next one we met the talking dog. I'm sure I've remembered it properly," he concluded.

Eldon could contain himself no longer: "Listen here you muscle bound, lame brained, over equipped example of a fighting man that talking dog was called 'The Entertainer'!" Thrugg absorbed this fresh item of information. Another conclusion was eventually reached: "We called him many things but none of them were 'The Entertainer'. I remember Gerald saying it was a flea bitten, fur coated, bag of ...." Gertrude decided to cut him off before he went any further.

"Thrugg," she said, "old friend. That 'Talking Dog' was a golem made by Springfever. After we'd got back to Sham from that mission - with Idaho mostly intact you'll remember - Eldon got in touch with Springfever. He was told that that particular golem was called 'The Entertainer'." There was another long, pensive, pause.

Thrugg started in pursuit of another thought: "But, if that *is* the case, why wasn't it entertaining?" he asked. Eldon started to formulate a considered, corrosive, empathetic, reply that destined never to be heard.

30

At that moment the door of the tavern burst open. The bright, midday, sunlight rush in to flood into every corner of the previously dark room. The shadows ran away to hide in the remoter and half seen corners. A small urchin like figure stood silhouetted in the doorway.

Rogo and the others recognised that this was Midge, Mudge the woodcutter's apprentice. Mudge used him to pick up the twigs and bind the small bundles of kindling that he sold with every stack of logs for the fire. The manner of Midge's entrance and the way he stood trembling with outstretched on the threshold proclaimed that he had news - and urgent news at that.

"He's coming!" he yelled as soon as everyone's attention was on him. And then he was gone. Nearly everyone else in the Inn went after him, rushing from the darkness into the bright, outdoor, light. Even Thrugg forsook his friends driven by the imperative tone of Midge's message.

Rogo looked around the tavern, blinking in the unaccustomed light. All that left were Eldon, Gertrude. Quickbeam, Gerald and himself. Everyone else had fled - either to hide somewhere else or to greet the 'him' whose arrival had been so spectacularly announced. Rogo caught Gerald's eye. The look they exchanged seem to say "Why not?"

Eldon was groping for the initiative. He began: "Rogo, who was Midge talking about and should we be worried? Is it time for us to hide in the cellar again?" Gerald saved his friend from the need of making something up. He addressed the table: "Shall we go and see for ourselves?" Standing he led the way from of the home comforts of "The Portly Pixie" and out into the inhospitable main street of Sham to see what was happening.

Chapter 4: A King Meets the People

Gerald led his friends out of the cool darkness of the inn. The sunlight hit them as they came out onto the street. It was not a pleasant feeling and their faces screwed up with the pain. Gertrude pulled her hood a little further over her eyes. Eldon held up a warding hand so as to produce a modicum of shade across his face. Gerald simply seemed to blend with the shadows no one else seemed able to find. Quickbeam drew out his spell book and started looking for a warding spell against the painful light. Thrugg met the challenge with his usual direct action. He glared up at the offending orb in the sky. It was if he was offering the sun a chance to come down and face him man to star. Remarkably the tactic worked and the sun retreated behind a small, fluffy, white cloud. The light got a little less painful and the adventurers moved on.

Rogo watched all this from the doorway of the inn. He shook his head slightly to himself, smiling as he saw Thrugg's victory. He was about to follow his friends when a thought struck him. Looking back into the darkness he could just make out the dim form of Skutlar still propping up the bar. "Stumpy!" he bellowed and the stand in orc cook burst in from the kitchen out back. He seemed to be wrestling with a small bear. Rogo ignored this, putting it down to an unusual "house special" and passed on the necessary instructions: "I'm stepping out for a few minutes. Keep an eye on Skutlar and make sure he doesn't drink all the profits." Rogo turned after receiving Stumpy's nod of acknowledgement. Then he paused once more. Turning back he added: "And Skutlar, make sure Stumpy pays for all his drinks as well." Receiving a grunt of acknowledgement from the recumbent figure, Rogo turned once more and moved out into the street.

As he looked up and down the hard packed dirt strip Rogo could see that there was a large crowd gathered. He anxiously searched the faces, looking for Eldon and the others. Where ever he looked he found a familiar face. Here was weather beaten face of Mudge the woodcutter, still clutching a bundle of freshly gathered sticks from the woods. Next to him was Fernlace the druid in his robes of an Elna priest just checking that Mudge had collected only dead wood. There was Tom the pawnbroker in deep conversation with several others. Objects were being exchanged for cash - typical of Tom to carry on working amid this chaos. Across the road stood a collection of priests who had obviously tumbled out of Mohan's Temple to All the Gods, setting aside their theological differences in the face of curiosity.

It was if the whole population of Sham had turned out to line the street. They were obviously waiting for something. There was a general air of expectation as if everyone knew what was going to happen. Rogo listened to the chit chat as he moved through the crowd. He had spotted Eldon and the rest so he headed towards the patch of shadow close to Eldon in which he knew his friend Gerald was standing.

Hamish MacAllen commented that not many like him came this way very often. Ogedei MacBoar replied that it was a long way from Battenburgh. Megan, one of Rogo's evening staff, wondered if there was something special about the way royalty smelt that made them so attractive. Samantha, who made a living by plying another trade, replied that she didn't really care as long as he was rich as all kings were. By the time Rogo reached Gerald he had put it all together.

"The King of Battenburgh is coming" Rogo said to no one in particular. "They call it a Royal Progress," Eldon informed him, drawing a smile from Gerald standing in the shadows. "Yes, I know," Rogo replied. "They bring a crowd of retainers who eat us out of house and home and leave chaos in their wake." "Sounds like my kind of guy," came a comment from the shadow wreathed Gerald. Everyone smiled at that - except Thrugg.

He was squinting down the street. His companions knew that he was thinking something through. In a moment he was going to reach one of his incisive conclusions. They were usually worth waiting for - so wait they did. Finally Thrugg spoke: "No. I can't see either of them". There was a pause while his friends waited for him to expand on the simple statement. Finally it fell to Gertrude to break the silence.

"Can't see either of whom?" she asked.

"I can't see a crowd of retainers with him nor that chaos bloke following along behind. It's just three men walking down the middle of the road," came the reply. There was another pause while Gertrude considered whether it was necessary to continue the conversation. She concluded that it simply was not going to be worth the effort and joined the others in looking down the dusty street to see just who was coming.

And, indeed, Thrugg was once more right with his simple statement. There were just three people walking towards the centre of Sham. Through the shimmering heat haze of the middle of the day that much was clear. They walked in a line, almost in step, purposefully towards the gathered crowd. The two that flanked the central figure were very similar in appearance. Both were tall, well built, and equipped like warriors. Each wore chain mail that twinkled in the sunlight. Each wore a black leather helmet on their head. They were clearly bodyguards.

And the tabards they wore over the mail coat proclaimed by the blue diamond over the traditional symbol of nobility that they were bodyguards of the royal house of Battenburgh. They walk with a pride and a swagger that showed they knew they

33

were the best of the best that that region could provide. Clearly the slightly smaller figure that walked between them was their charge. This was the royal personage whose progress into the centre of the village they were protecting. And he, too, deserved closer inspection.

He wore no trappings of a warrior. He had no armour and carried no weapons. A soft, black, velvet cap graced his head instead of leather protection. In fact most of the clothes he wore were black. The silk shirt, the linen trousers and even the obligatory accessories of gloves and boots were black. The depth of the colour told anyone who knew anything about clothing that these clothes had never been washed. Nor would they be. Having been worn they would be discarded so that the perfection of their blackness would not be disrupted by the slight fading caused by the application of soap and water.

As he continued to come closer it became clearer that the black clothes were accented by those little touches of finery that confirmed this man had wealth. There were red and white trimmings on boots and gloves showing they had both been hand stitched to a high standard. And the occasional glint of golden yellow from shirt cuff and front showed that he was a person of rank. This was confirmed by the greater golden glint coming from around his head. Here the sunlight was reflecting off the simple crown worn over the leather cap. Even at a distance anyone looking at him could see that he was every inch a King. And the people of Sham, including the small group of adventurers, knew this too.

Gerald had already calculated the value of the treasure on view, worked out how to steal most of it, decided how to conceal his choice of the items from his comrades, calculated how much Rogo would be prepared to pay him for those pieces and what he would buy with this unexpected windfall.

These deliberations were interrupted when one of the more easily impressed villagers - Rockhead the stone breaker from the quarry supplying the castle - gave voice to his emotions with a loud shout of "Long live the King!". The small royal procession was brought to a sudden stop by the King. Rogo looked at his friend Gerald and they considered whether an insult had been given and taken by their regal guest. They both became a little more nervous as the king stretched out his hand to the bodyguard that stood on his right. Was a weapon to be taken and royal prerogative exercised with immediate justice? How should Rogo and the others react then? After all, this was their turf and, if immediate justice was to be metered out, they were the ones that were going to do it. Rogo knew that Gerald and he could take all of them as there were only three of them. But one of them was a king - and what would Zama say when she got back?

The bodyguard standing to the right of the kingly figure reached towards his belt. Rogo and Gerald both tensed as they waited for the weapon to be drawn. That's when the trouble would start and it would be time to be somewhere else. Luckily it was not a sword that was taken from the belt and placed in the king's hand. It was a leather purse. Gerald and Rogo relaxed a little but remained alert until they saw what the purse contained. They did not have long to wait.

Still looking at Rockhead who had proclaimed a long life to his majesty, the king drew something out of the purse. He immediately threw it to the man. It spun and sparkled silver in the air before being plucked into safety by the quarry worker. There was another moment of tension as Rockhead surveyed what he had been given. The crowd was silent. The royal procession was still. Even Rogo and Gerald hardly dare draw breath until they knew what was going on.

Rockhead slowly looked up from his hands and stared straight at the king. His eyes were wide and his jaw hung loose. He was obviously in deep shock. The king smiled back at him - although the smile seemed to lack warmth to the trained eye. The stone breaker looked down at the coin he held once more. He carefully examined it. It was silver and bore in raised relief a picture of an owl. If possible it seemed that Rockhead's eyes got even wider - as if the disbelief had just got deeper. He tentatively placed the coin between his teeth in the traditional manner to test its quality. It passed and he once more looked wide eyed at it lying on his palm. Finally, from somewhere deep behind the eyes wide open a thought reached the vocal chords and he spoke:

"Fifty beans!"

The silence surrounding this mini drama that had just been acted out on the village street grew deeper as this extra datum was absorbed by the crowd. The king acknowledged this somewhat unconventional expression of thanks with a slight nod of the head. And then all hell broke loose. Everyone was shouting and praising their royal visitor. The cacophony grew louder as the king responded with a scattering of coins in all directions. Movement was added to the chorus of praise as people began scrambling on their hands and knees on the street in a desperate rush to collect what they clearly saw as their coins.

Rogo and his friend Gerald watched this chaos with a certain detachment. They didn't need the odd fifty beans - or at least they weren't going to be seen grovelling for it on the streets. In the end Rogo felt that he had to say something. "The things people will do for money!" he said, to no-one in particular. There was a slight pause as Gerald ran through a check list in his head of the things he had done for fifty beans - most of them illegal or, in the least of dubious merit. Then it penetrated what Rogo was going on about. "Yes," he replied, again to no-one in particular, "look at Gez over there. And Rogo turned to look in the direction indicated by his friend.

Gez, the goblin, was desperately scrambling for the scattered coins. As Rogo watched he dived into the midden heap next to the side door of 'The Portly Pixie' to emerge a few moments later with his furs all covered with choice pieces of dung. Strangely his clothes seemed a little cleaner than when he had dived into the heap in the first place. But then Gez was not known for his cleanliness. He was triumphantly clutching the metal disc of his pursuit. Both watchers winced as he popped the coin into his mouth to suck it clean before it was added to his bulging pouch. Nothing went into that pouch unless it was clean. That was one of the many peculiarities of the goblin Gez. Having trapped that prey he was off amongst the feet for more that was still raining down from the king's hand.

Rogo and Gerald watched fascinated by this frantic coin collecting behaviour. They were intrigued as Gez, on his hands and knees, came to a sudden stop. He encountered a foot that had been unthinkingly and inconsiderately placed on the next coin that clearly belonged to Gez. The goblin turned his eyes upwards to look with derision at the man who have the temerity to obstruct his latest wealth collection activity. And the goblin found himself looking eye to eye with what was clearly a thug. It was Gez who lost that battle of the stares. Defeated by the solid stare he finally withered under the gaze of the thug and scrambled away.

Gerald and Rogo, while amused by this, were wary of the arrival of this stranger in the village street. At first glance there was nothing special about him. His clothes were no different from any other travel worn peasant who frequently passed through Sham. From dusty cloak to muddy boots he was clearly a traveller. But there was something about the way he had stared down Gez and stood, with his hand on his sword hilt, that rang alarm bells in the watchers minds. They watched as the thug turned his attention to the King walking along the street. They become a little more alert as they noticed that the thug was not alone. Four more stood close to him. They were similarly anonymous but with that not quite hidden menace. They had ranged themselves in a loose formation and they were all watching the king. Once more the two friends prepared themselves for action. Gerald even went so far as to try and alert his companions but Eldon was too busy looking for the odd unclaimed coin to listen.

As the royal party came closer to the main body of the crowd the five thugs seemed to prepare themselves for some imminent action. Rogo moved alongside Gerald in what shadow there was. They stood silent and still. Only their eyes showed any movement - and that was almost imperceptible. To anyone but a close observer they seemed to have simply faded from sight. They were watching the strangers, and the strangers were watching the king and his bodyguards.

As the royal party came closer it was clearly time for action. The leader of the thugs, the one who had had the staring match with Gez, made a slight nod with his head. He and his companions began to move from the side of the street, pushing through the few who stood in their way. They stood in the middle of the road to confront the king. The king's bodyguards moved to stand in front of their charge. The thugs struck first and the bodyguards were both lying on the ground. "That was nice cosh work," Gerald whispered to his shadow companion. Rogo's slightest nod indicated that he had heard and concurred. His eyes never left the unfolding action.

Having dealt with the hired help the bandits, as they were now clearly seen to be, moved on to face the man who had hired the now sleeping guards. Once more a cosh rose and fell with lightning speed. It was the king who was now lying face down in the dust. As two of the thugs bent down to scope him up the others were warily watching the crowd. They had their hands on their sword hilts. That was enough to deter those who were not scrambling for the loose coins from making an intervention. The thugs simply and efficiently had taken the king prisoner by force. Carrying their burden, they made off up the street and out of Sham into the woods beyond.

Most of the crowd simply hadn't seen anything. Those who had noticed the recent events reacted by shrugging their shoulders. No king in their minds meant no more free coins so it was time to go. Most of the villagers decided it was time to get out of the sun and go back to whatever it was they were doing before this year's excitement began. Not even Eldon had witnessed what had come to pass. He was still desperately trying to gather in a twenty bean coin that had chosen a particularly sticky piece of horse dung to settle in. Finally he managed it without too much muck getting on his gloves and stood up in triumph.

Looking up and down the street he took in the scene. Rogo and Gerald now watching him from the shadows thought they could hear the cogs turning in his brain. Look at street. Notice lack of people. Look up and down the street. Still no people. Notice the two bodyguards still lying unconscious in the dust. Look up and down the street again - looking particularly for their missing boss. And frame the question. With perfect timing Rogo and Gerald joined in with the chorus led by Eldon: "Where's the King?"

Eldon glared in the direction of the shadows. He was obviously formulating a cutting put down before Thrugg spoke and further distracted him: "Five men took him that way," he said pointing to the woods that lay by the side of the Battenburgh road. Now Eldon's attention was fixed on Thrugg. He was waiting for him to expand on the simple statement and fill him in on the missing events of the last few moments. It was clear to everyone except Eldon that he was in for a very long wait. As usual it fell to Gertrude to expand upon their friends simple, factual, statement.

"Five men. Professionals by their cosh work. Took out the bodyguards - and then the king. Went that-a-way with him. The crowd's gone because no king means no money. Clear now? You've caught up?"

Eldon took a few moments to absorb the concise summary of the events. "Caught up," he confirmed after this period of reflection. Rogo and Gerald stepped out of the shadows and joined their friends. "That's that, then," said Rogo, turning to lead his friends back into the cool darkness of the inn. "But ..." Eldon stammered. Rogo stopped and turned to look at him once more. The look said it all - come on, I've got work to do. Once more Eldon struggled to find the right words and came up with only: "But ..." Now it was Rogo's turn to speak.

"You've said that already. I've got work to do. So but what Eldon my friend?" he demanded. Eldon took a moment and this time was able to frame the question: "What about the king?" Rogo stared his friend in the eyes. He then turned to look up and down the now mainly empty street, squinting finally in the direction that the prostrate king had been unceremoniously carried. He return his attention to Eldon having reached his conclusion: "Not my problem". Rogo turned and strode from the oven heat of the street into the comfort of his inn.

Gerald eased himself off the wall. "That's that, then," he said to no one in particular. He followed the landlord into his inn. The other members of the adventuring band moved after him. They left Eldon standing alone in the sunlight. He was frantically looking around for someone to support him as he plaintively bleated "But ... But .... But ..." to anyone who could hear - which was no one.

Back inside the inn Rogo had made his way behind the bar table. He nodded to Stumpy who gratefully made his way back into the kitchen. Skutlar was still head down and once more insensible at the end of the table. Sighing to himself Rogo started to pour a round of drinks for his adventuring chums joining him at the table. They were happy to spend the next few minutes quenching the thirst that the noon day sun had induced in them. Suddenly Thrugg came out with another of his simple earth shattering statements: "I can hear something."

Everyone stopped drinking and listened hard. From outside the inn door came a small voice repeating one word over and over again: "But ... But ... But ..." Gertrude explained what her friend had heard: "It's Eldon. He's confused - or possibly suffering from sunstroke. Go and get him Thrugg." Her over muscled companion turned away from the bar and went out onto the street once more. Quickbeam looked up from the book he had been reading. He peered at Gertrude over the top of his glasses:

"You know what he's going to do, don't you?" Gertrude nodded. Quickbeam continued: "And you did that on purpose, didn't you?" Once more Gertrude nodded.

The inn door burst open. Thrugg was returning. Thrugg was carrying Eldon easily in front of him. He brought his leader to the bar and placed him in front of his favourite drink that Rogo had already poured. Sensing the alcohol Eldon finally stopped repeated his single word. He reached out for the drink to down it in one. Rogo echoed the earlier words of his friend "So, that's that then," and turned to get another flask from the back table.

He immediately wished he hadn't for Eldon started up once more: "But ... But ... But ... " Patiently Rogo asked him "But what Eldon?" The reply was the familiar stammering: "But ... But ... But ..." Rogo lifted his eyes to the ceiling in frustration. He turned to the back bar and selected a bottle of his favourite strong spirit. He poured himself a beaker of it. The others sensed that if Eldon didn't do something soon about his speech impediment, Rogo would. And it wouldn't be pretty. And Eldon wouldn't like it. Once more it fell to Gertrude to save the day.

She took Eldon firmly by the shoulders and turned him to look at her. She stared directly into his eyes. When she was sure that she had his attention she said emphatically "For crying out loud, Eldon. Stop with the goat impressions and get on with it - whatever it is you're trying to say!" The glazed look seemed to leave Eldon's eyes as the words bored their way through the confusion. He blinked and turned from Gertrude to once more confront Rogo as they stood on opposite sides of the bar table. Eldon was still having difficulties in forming exactly what it was he wanted to say. Then he noticed the beaker of spirit on the bar before him.

He took it in his right hand and drained it in a single draft. The contents had a remarkable effect on Eldon. He reacted as if he had been hit with a club. Gerald said it was as if smoke came out of his ears. After a moment's immobility Eldon shook himself. He was himself once more and, taking a deep breath, confronted Rogo with the dilemma that had driven him into immobility.

"Rogo," he said accusingly, " Are you or are you not the law in this region?" Rogo wondered for a second what Zama would say about that before confirming his status with a nod of the head. Eldon continued: "And haven't you just witnessed - along with my reliable colleagues and myself - a crime committed in the street outside your front door?" Rogo took another moment to consider this. It was the word 'reliable' he was having problems with. In the end he decided that it was not worth splitting hairs at this stage of the conversation. It might just start off the goat impressions again!

39

Instead he confined his reply to the single word "Yes".

Eldon was suddenly very pleased with himself. He straightened up and look around the inn. Addressing no one in particular he announced his success at apparently trapping Rogo into admitting something highly significant: "There we are. I told you so." Then he turned once more to face Rogo with what was obviously the point of all this: "And so, what are you going to do about it?"

Rogo reached forward and picked up the now empty beaker from the bar table. He plunged it into the bowl of water beneath the table and began to dry it on his cloth. Eldon watched, his impatience growing. However, his self control had partially returned and he knew that Rogo was drawing out the moment for effect. So he waited to see what Rogo was going to say.

Rogo could see Eldon getting more and more agitated. Gerald and Gertrude were clearly enjoying the moment as well. Once the beaker was dry Rogo turned and replaced in along the spirit bottles on the back bar. He turned back to Eldon and gave him what was clearly a considered reply: "Absolutely nothing." Eldon's flabber was well and truly gasted. All he could do was to repeat what Rogo had said - "Nothing?" - before once more embarking again on a seemingly endless stream of "But ... But ... But ..."

Gerald brought this to a stop with his comment of "He's making with the goats again!" Eldon spun around to glare at him - and that had absolutely no effect beyond restoring Eldon's senses once more. Gerald simply continued to lean against the table he was next to smiling to himself and to anyone else who cared to look in his direction. Eldon was forced once more to turn and confront Rogo behind the bar.

Drawing himself up to his full height, squaring his shoulders and making himself look as much as if he was in control as possible, Eldon looked Rogo straight in the eye. Rogo calmly continued to clean the tankards and goblets with the not so clean cloth. In the end Eldon's resolve was complete. He handed out his instructions: "Rogo, you have to do something." Rogo continued to meet Eldon's stare with an air of quiet contemplation. It looked as if he was considering the action that he was going to take from the range of alternatives that presented themselves in his mind. And this was going to take a few moments.

The moments became jiffies, the jiffies became a minute or two and it seemed to be stretching towards an age. Eldon could contain himself no longer. Once more he spoke with assumed authority: "Now." Rogo stopped his cleaning and decisively placed cloth and tankard onto the bar table. He was now giving Eldon his full attention. And Eldon knew it. Second by second as Rogo looked deeply into his eyes Eldon could feel his confidence seeping away. He tried once more to speak with self-belief, only for the voice to betray him. "Please?" came out more as a squeak than a bellow.

Eldon's squeak had sounded like a mouse and Rogo's reaction was as quick as any cat cornering the same rodent. "Why," he said quietly but firmly. Eldon knew who was in charge now and struggled for an answer. Rogo lifted a hand to make him pause and continued: "I know what you're going to say. 'Because he is a King and Kings have to ransomed'." Eldon nodded weakly in confirming acknowledgement. Rogo went on: "But he's not the King of Chouse. And I see no threat to the town or region of Sham - which is the area that I am in charge of policing. So I intend to do nothing. In any case where's the profit in rescuing a King?"

Having completed his statement of opinion, Rogo picked up his cloth. He was making ready to resume his cleaning routine. As far as he was concerned the discussion was over. Gertrude thought so too saying: "That's that then. Now, who's for afternoon tea?" But Eldon would not let it go. He had to try once more: "You've got to do something," he demanded. Those words had a profound effect on the local inn keeper cum law officer.

It also stirred Gerald into rapid movement away from the immediate area of Eldon. He had seen Rogo lay down his cleaning cloth once more - but this time with exasperated force. He also saw Rogo's right hand slide underneath the bar table. Gerald knew that Rogo kept a small club there for times such as these - and it looked likely that Eldon was going to feel the blunt end of it. Gerald was moving out of the way because Rogo didn't lose his temper very often these days, but it was a good idea to be somewhere else when he did!

However, even this potentially traumatic moment was to be overtaken by other events. There was a breaking of glass. Pieces of the pane of the small window to the left of the door scattered themselves onto the floor. The cause of this unexpected breakage was a brick. Following this dramatic entrance it was flying across the inn's common room heading directly for Eldon's head. Gerald found himself wondering how Rogo had arranged for this as, in a matter of seconds, the brick had struck its target and Eldon was pole-axed. He fell to the floor ending in a crumpled heap in front of the bar table. The brick nestled against his head.

Rogo surveyed the prone figure. "That's that, then," he commented to no-one in particular. "I'm grateful to whoever threw this brick to shut him up - but they're still going to pay for the window." Rogo stalked out from behind the bar and started to head for the inn door. Thrugg was ahead of him. He had already pulled open the door and was staring out into the sun lit street. "And people think he's slow!", Rogo thought to himself as he made his way in Thrugg's direction. Gertrude's voice stopped him: "Rogo," she said, "there's a note on this brick."

Now Rogo's attention was hooked - maybe it was an order for take away food or beer. They'd be profit in that! "Read it," he instructed, not taking this eyes off the street outside. Gertrude bent to obey. Removing the note from the brick she unfolded it. She read: "We've got the King. Bring 1000 beans and no weapons or we send him back - one little piece at a time." Rogo considered these orders. He had clearly made up his mind as he said: "Now I **will** do something!" He crossed back to the bar. There he bent and lifted the senseless head of Eldon. With two swift slaps and "Wake up, sleeping beauty" he brought Eldon out of his brick induced sleep. "What hit me?" Eldon enquired.

"Well, it was me - after the brick, of course," Rogo gently informed him. "Now, try and stand up." The unsteady Eldon was helped to his feet by the determined inn keeper. "Raise your right hand and repeat after me," the instructions continued. The half dazed Eldon obeyed as Rogo administered an oath familiar to all: "I Eldon do hereby agree to serve as magistrate in the region known as Sham and carry out such law keeping duties that might be required of me by the Thanes of that region." Parrot like, and obviously more aware on the bump on the side of his head than what he was saying, Eldon talked himself into become a magistrate. Once the oath had been completed Rogo guided Eldon to a nearby stool. There he gently seated him before giving him his first set of instructions in his new office.

"You have been on at me to do something about the kidnapping of the King. I have decided on a course of action. I'm making it your problem. Sort it out by sunset or else." Rogo stalked off in the direction of the kitchen. Gerald wondered - but had the sense not to ask - what the 'or else' might be. Rogo had one more parting shot before leaving the scene. He turned back and fired one last instruction at his newly appointed assistant: "And find out who broke my window!" The kitchen door slammed shut to mark Rogo's exit.

There was a short moment of stillness in the common room. In their separate ways the occupants were taking in the events of the last few minutes. Eldon was clearly working out what had happened to him. In his dazed condition it was taking him a few moments to catch up. Gerald was watching him carefully. He wanted to see the moment the one bean coin dropped. Thrugg was still standing in the doorway looking up the street. Gertrude looked to their leader, patiently waiting for his instructions. Quickbeam began leafing through his spell book, selecting the ones that might be needed in the near future. Skutlar slept on, head still down on the bar table as if nothing had happened. Of course, from his point of view nothing had!

In the end Eldon had caught up. He leapt into action - only to sit down again immediately as the dizziness overcame him. Gertrude went over him, all maternal. "There, there, dear," she said, stroking his fevered brow, "You just sit there and tell us what you'd like us to do to help you in your new position." Gerald was the only one who heard the irony in her voice and smiled to himself. Eldon considered carefully before replying: "First, we have to find out where that brick came from!"

From the door way Thrugg provided an answer: "A man threw it." That was almost too much for Eldon who, leaping to his feet, stormed across the room to confront his over muscled subordinate. Face to face Eldon virtually spat out: "That's a fat lot of good. There must be hundreds of men out there who could have thrown it. How does that help?" Thrugg drew himself up to his full height and towered over his leader. The others wondered if this was going to be the one sided fight they'd all been expecting for days now. But no, it was just Thrugg's way of gathering his thoughts.

After a pause, he spoke: "There's no need to shout at me Eldon. I didn't get Rogo cross with all the goat impressions and I know that brick must have hurt you when it hit. But I didn't throw it. As I told you, a man did. And despite what you think there are not hundreds of men out there. In fact since the brick was thrown there have been never more than six people in the street at any one time. And only one of them has been there all the time. He's the one loitering down by Uncle Tom's Cabin. And I suspect by the furtive glances he keeps making in this direction, that he's the one who threw the brick."

Eldon dived to the doorway. "Which one?" he barked. Thrugg favoured him with an answer to the question that Eldon hadn't asked: "Uncle Tom's Cabin is the pawn brokers on the Battenburgh road where we go when Rogo and Zama don't think some of the stuff we've brought home is worth as much you do. It's that black and white building with the bars on all the windows and the three brass orbs hanging outside." Eldon closed his eyes in frustration. He took a moment to gather his thoughts. It was clear that he was about to plunge into even deeper uncharted waters when Gertrude stepped in to save the moment: "Thrugg. Eldon is asking which man you think threw the brick."

Thrugg pointed with his tree trunk arms: "That one".

By now all the adventurers had gathered in the doorway. They followed the line of Thrugg's arm. Where the finger was pointing stood a non-descript, ordinary looking man. He was no taller than Eldon and had a slim build. He appeared to have been painted in a mixture of unmatched brown. He wore a simple, sackcloth shirt of one hue and homespun trousers of another tucked into short boots of a third. The shirt was belted at the waist and he carried no obvious weapons. All that hung from the belt was a small, half empty cloth purse. He wore a hood of yet another shade of brown that was over his head, protecting him from the sun. However, his face was visible from the inn doorway. Gerald thought to himself that it reminded him of a weasel, except for the thick, black, rat of a moustache fixed to his upper lip. His eyes were never still, flitting this way and that. But suddenly he knew that he was being watched for they looked directly at the doorway of the inn. For a moment his two eyes met the ten that were directed towards him, He broke that contact and started to search for a way out of the mess he had found himself in.

Eldon took this as a sign that he was going to have to do something. That meant the others were going to have to help as well. With the instruction; "Come on" he strode out of the inn and once more down the sun baked street. Taking the lead from Gerald's shrug of the shoulders, the others followed. They fell naturally into their careful, alert marching order. Within moments they were gathered in a loose group around a frightened rabbit of a man standing outside Uncle Tom's Cabin.

Even though he was leaning nonchalantly against the wall of the pawn shop, it was clear the brick throwing thug was not happy. He had a way of looking all around him but never catching any of the eyes of the small group of heroes that had come to confront him. Gerald thought that at any moment now he was going to be off - and it was probably going to be Gerald that was going to have to bring him back! Eldon's bombastic manner didn't help either. From the start it was clear that the conversation was not going to go well.

Eldon began: "Now my good man ... " and the thug turned sharply to face the newly appointed magistrate. He gave Eldon a look of pure hatred which was sufficient to bring the rest of the opening statement to a stop. There was a moment of real tension. The thug seemed to be trying to decide which bit of Eldon he was going to eat first. Eldon became very nervous and his right hand started to twitch towards his sword.

It was the thug that broke the tension: "I wouldn't do that if I were you," he said. After a short pause for effect he continued: "Because I'm not your - or anyone else's – 'good' man." He coughed and carefully aimed a drop of spittle to land directly between Eldon's feet. Eldon reacted by moving back a couple of paces. To Gerald looking on it was if he was more concerned about getting his boots dirty than addressing the insult that had been dealt to him. It fell, as usual, to Gertrude to take over the negotiations.

"He didn't mean anything by it. It's just his way," she began. "Now, let's get on with it. We got your brick. Give us the King and we'll give you your money." This brought an instant reaction from the thug. "Not so fast," he snapped in reply.

"Am I going too fast for you?" Gertrude responded sweetly. "Let me talk a little slower then .."

"That's enough of that," came the retort, "I'm not as stupid as I look. You're not going to even see the King until I've seen the money. And you can lose those weapons as well. There's nothing you can do about it. Without me you'll never find him and I've got my orders and I'm going to stick to them."

Gertrude thought for a moment. "O.K. then," she said finally, "What is it exactly that you want us to do?"

The thug smiled in triumph. Gerald smiled in recognition of the ease by which Gertrude had hoodwinked him into thinking he had won. Gertrude smiled in encouragement and the thug began to lay out his terms: "First, you're to go back to the inn and leave all your weapons inside. Rogo will look after them and that way I'll know I'm safe. Then you're to get the money - all 1000 beans of it - and bring it for me to see. And then I'll take you to where the King is being held. We can do the exchange and everyone will be happy."

The adventurers looked one to another as they absorbed what they had heard. It didn't take them long to come to unspoken agreement as to what should happen next. Almost as one they turned to retrace their steps up the main street of Sham and back to the inn. Thrugg was left to speak for them. He towered over the thug as he made the parting statement: "We'll be back". The thug was noticeably relieved when the inn door slammed behind his tormentors - but, of course, there was no-one left to see his relaxation.

Rogo was back cleaning - well, wiping at least - the tankards when his crack troop of adventurers made their way back into the common room. He looked up and quickly counted heads. "That was quick," he observed before asking: "Where's the King?" There was a short pause before Gertrude once more was pushed forward to lead the group's negotiations. "Rogo," she began, her voice dripping with sugar, honey and all manner of other sweetness.

Rogo knew when he was beaten. He raised the not so white towel he held in his right hand. "I surrender, Gertrude," he said. "Just tell me what you need and we'll get down to the business of agreeing terms." Gertrude looked from one to another of her friends to get their agreement before recounting to Rogo their plight and her solution to it.

It was only a few minutes later that the band of would be rescuers once more left the inn to approach the thug who still waited by Uncle Tom's Cabin at the far end of the village. Gerald was amazed that even having seemingly given ground at the opening, Rogo had still managed to negotiate a tenth share of any treasure resulting from the forthcoming quest in exchange for the loan - he had been adamant about that bit - of a large sack of cabbages. But at least to outside eyes the sack was doing the job. Gerald's professional eye could see that the thug was assessing this new situation quite carefully as they approached. He also saw that their deception had worked.

From the thug's point of view the small band of warriors who now approached him were completely unarmed. They had heeded his instructions to leave all their weapons in the inn. They were also carrying what was obviously a very heavy sack. Surely this contained the 1000 beans that had been demanded. The thug was certain that he had got his way.

But not everything was as it seemed. The sack still contained the cabbages that were in it when Rogo had hired to Gertrude and the rest. That was what was giving it the weight. The same sack also concealed most of the party's weapons. Thrugg's broadsword had proved to be a problem until Gerald had suggested stuffing it down his tunic. Thrugg was now walking very stiffly and very carefully to avoid injuring himself. Despite appearances, the group was still ready for action. And the bandits were not going to get their 1000 beans!

"Right," Eldon said to the thug, back in instructive mode, "Let's go get the King." "Show me the cash," the thug retorted. Thrugg held the sack in front of the thug's nose. The ease with which Thrugg handled the heavy sack made the thug go pale about the gills. Looking nervously up at the warrior the thug was aware of a pained expression on Thrugg's face. "What's the matter with him?" he asked no-one in particular.

"Touch of back ache" explained Gertrude, after a moment's pause. Gerald had to fake a coughing fit to cover the laughter that rose unbidden in his throat. "And he's got a cold," Gertrude went on to explain while turning her back on the thug to glare at her near hysterical companion. Her look was enough to banish any thought of mirth from Gerald's mind for the rest of the day!

The thug was certain he was missing something. He looked slowly from adventurer to adventurer. He couldn't find anything to give a firmer foundation to his suspicions and so he was forced into the inevitable conclusion: "Come on, then," he said, turning to lead the would be rescuers out of the village and into the wild woods that surround it. He even had the confidence to whistle to himself as he led the expedition that was a good thing. The noise of his whistling meant he missed Thrugg's comment, to no-one in particular, that he didn't have back ache and his question as to when had Gerald caught his cold.

But the adventurers were confident as well. They would rescue the King and return victorious to the village. They would be laden with treasure. Rogo would greet them to take his ten percent - and to reclaim his cabbages. But that would not matter for the King would shower them with honours. They were about to spend the rest of their lives on easy street.

As events were about to unfold, though, their confident hopes were mostly to remain unfulfilled. For example, Rogo was never going to get his cabbages back. And that was the least of their worries in the woods beyond Sham!

Chapter 5: A Walk in the Woods

The sun was shining as the bold adventurers left the comparative safety of the village. They moved from the full glare of its rays into the dappled shade of the fringe of the woodland trees. Very soon they were hemmed in on all sides. Threats could hide behind every tree, ambushers could lurk in every shadow and danger could skulk behind every bush. But this was a familiar place for our heroes and they fell easily into a well tried routine.

Immediately behind their guide walked Thrugg. It was clear that the bandit's spokesman was not happy about this. He took every step as if it was his last. "Any minute," he was thinking to himself, "that muscled bound oaf is going to trip up and land right on top of me." As they entered the woods the guide had even suggested to Thrugg that he go first. There was a long pause as the question was considered. Finally an answer came: "No". The word could have been carved in stone for the weight it carried. The guide's shoulders had sagged, knowing he would have to lead the party. Thrugg's further explanation: "I do not know the way" only added to his gloom. The unwilling guide was not a happy bunny.

Thrugg on the other hand was delighted to be out amongst the trees again. This was where he felt at home. For one thing there was plenty of headroom. It was not like the cottages and other buildings in Sham where he nearly always had to move with a slight stoop so as to avoid damaging the ceilings. And there was plenty of room between the trees. His massive bulk could pass with ease between their trunks as they followed the well used path. It was not like the time he got stuck trying to get out of the back door of the inn because he forgot to turn sideways. And he knew where he was going - following the bloke in front. He didn't have to do anything about choosing the way and this left him time to look around. Even that was a pleasure because this close to the village there was rarely any threats. Yes. Thrugg had time to watch the rabbits, birds and other small creatures who scampered away from their somewhat noisy passage.

Immediately behind the two members of the advance guard strode Eldon. As befitted the leader of the band he had to be near the front. His head was held high to give the impression that he was in charge. He walked with confidence to show that he knew where he was going. His chain mail sparkled in the sunlight revealing him to be a man of substance. This all went to show that appearances can be deceptive. Eldon had no more idea than Thrugg where they were going. He, too, was simply following their bandit leader. As for the scampering creatures, they were a source of constant concern for him. He would never forget the time he broke his ankle tripping over a fleeing rabbit. His every step was full of apprehension.

Quickbeam and Gertrude followed in their usual places just behind their leader. It would seem that this put the necessary reserves close to their leader so that he could efficiently deploy them. Here the magical support of the wizard could be quickly brought to bear on any danger while Gertrude, the healer, was ready to get on with patching up any damaged members of the party. At the heart of the small band they were also offered the protection of Eldon who would quickly overcome any threat to them. However, once more appearances conspired to deceive.

Quickbeam and Gertrude were where they were to keep an eye on Eldon. If anyone was likely to need help it was going to be him - and Gertrude was forever having to patch him up. Neither of them was enjoying this journey. Usually they shared some measure of control of their situation. But this time they were having to trust their guide as they continued into what they knew was hostile territory. Both knew that those nearest the front were the most likely to get hurt. That meant that at any time they might lose their guide - so Gertrude was ready to patch him up as well if necessary.

Bringing up the rear of this band was their normal scout. Denied of his usual vanguard position, Gerald had taken over as the rear guard. He was not happy. It wasn't that he disliked being at the back - it was that he didn't like having to appear unarmed. His normal confidence was reinforced with a short sword and his throwing daggers readily to hand. Now they were some 20 feet away in the sack of cabbages hanging over Thrugg's left shoulder. Seemingly so totally disarmed made him nervous. His eyes were never still as he scanned the woods for danger. Seeing nothing made him even more nervous. He suspected a surprise attack at any moment. Gerald was jumping at every movement in the undergrowth.

Gertrude sensed the unease behind her. It was disturbing her concentration - and her enjoyment of the quiet walk in the woods. She could feel the tension building in her and knew that she was going to have to do something. She stopped and turned round to face her rearguard companion. Gerald didn't notice this. He was so busy watching a bush intently on the right hand side. He was sure he'd seen it move a few moments ago. He was so worried about the possibility of a hidden assassin that he walked straight into the stationary Gertrude. Gerald spun around in an instant, groping for the sword that wasn't there. Finally he recognised his friend and relaxed a little.

"Will you just stop it!" Gertrude hissed fiercely in his face. "But that bush moved," Gerald offered as a lame excuse. Gertrude squinted in the direction indicated before giving her considered opinion: "It's probably the wind. Why can't you just enjoy a quiet walk in the woods for a change?" Gerald looked down at his boots which were stirring the dust at his feet. Gertrude thought that he looked every inch the petulant child being made to do the necessary chores. Gertrude knew there was something else bothering her friend. "What has got into you?" she demanded.

There was a long pause as Gerald stirred up some more dust. Gertrude was tempted to clip him round the ear. Before she let that impulse get the better of her Gerald spoke: "Don't like being unarmed, " he said, raising his head to meet her eyes, "It's dangerous!" The look of desperation in his eyes made Gertrude smile inside. She reached out her right hand and placed it gently on his shoulder.

"You know and I know that you are not unarmed," she said in a comforting voice. "If I guess right you have a dagger in each boot, another in the middle of your back and a pair of throwing daggers - one on each forearm. So you're not unarmed." She took her hand off his shoulder. "So pull yourself together," she snapped.

She turned and caught up the rest of the party who had got a little bit ahead of her. Gerald was left a little bit further behind, still watching the bushes as he stirred the dust with his boots. He looked down the narrow path through the trees along which his friends were disappearing into the distance. Suddenly, he stopped stirring the dust and his senses switched into overdrive. He knew where the guide was taking them - and it was not the best way to go. He had to do something. He hurried down the road after Gertrude and the rest.

As he joined her the party was emerging from the woods onto the side of hill which was bare of trees. Gerald arrived in a rush at Gertrude's right hand side. He desperately tugged at her sleeve. "I know where we're going!" he hissed. "So do I," Gertrude replied patiently. "We're following our guide to go and rescue a King." Gerald shook his head. "That's not what I mean," he hissed more urgently. Gertrude looked at him and realised that this was one of those rare moments when Gerald was showing real concern.

Before the conversation could continue Quickbeam had walked into the back of Eldon who had walked into the back of Thrugg. Their guide heard the commotion of colliding bodies and stopped himself. Turning around he wondered what was going on. Two of those who were following lay in a heap at the rear of the biggest while the other two seemed to be in deep and earnest conversation about who was going to pick who up. "Why have we stopped?" he demanded. Thrugg provided the answer.

"We shouldn't be here," he said in his usual slow, considered way. The guide digested this as if the ponderous words needed weighing one by one in order to make any sense of them. In the end he knew he was going to have to ask for more information before he could make sense of what appeared to be a simple sentence. "Look," he said, "If you expect to see your King alive again, then you've got to be here. I'm the one who's leading you to where we are holding him and you've got to follow me."

Close behind this conversational confrontation Eldon and Quickbeam were slowly picking themselves up. Looking around the empty landscape and at one another they could make no sense of what was unfolding before them. Eldon looked quizzically at Quickbeam who shrugged his shoulders. It was clear that he had no idea what was going on either. Eldon straightened himself in readiness to demand further explanations from the slow discussion unfolding before him. Before he could speak he was frozen into inactivity as a hand was placed on his shoulder. He turned slowly to see who had restrained him.

He found himself looking straight into the gentle eyes of Gertrude who seem to be saying that he should wait and see. Thrugg normally got there in the end and it was often fun to watch others struggle with his literal way of analysing any situation. With a slight nod of acknowledgement, Eldon turned back to watch the fun.

Much to the exasperation of their thug guide, Thrugg was thinking. As usual this was taking some time and the bandit was slowly burning with the frustration. Finally a conclusion was reached and Thrugg delivered his deciision: "I don't have to follow you. It is true that we don't know where you are taking us but I have decided that you don't know where you are going. You must be a stranger around here for you have led us into the heart of an area where you will find lots and lots of aggressive ...."

Gerald, from the rear of the party, finished the sentence for him with a cry of "Orcs!". Thrugg turned slowly to look at his rude friend. "There's no need to shout," he chided. "It's not like there's a couple of them creeping up on us as we stand here."

"No," Gerald countered. "There's not a couple of orcs creeping up on us - there's a load of them streaming down that hill over there!" Thrugg, along with the rest of the party turned to look in the direction Gerald had indicated. Sure enough an orc war band had appeared and was charging towards the heroes. They were still some distance away but the manner in which they were waving their weapons and the grunts and snarls being carried on the wind showed their hostile intent. Thrugg narrowed his eyes and from the pained expression on his face, it was clear he was having a problem with some task.

The orcs were getting closer and closer and still Thrugg was occupied in his task. Finally his conclusion was reached and he announced: "There's not loads of them, Gerald. I make it 34." He paused, waiting for a comment from his friend. None came.

Turning slowly he enquired "Gerald?" and the reason for the silence became clear. Gerald was leading the charge from the open spaces of the heath back into the cover of the trees. The rest of the party were also running for their lives - including their bandit guide. Thrugg was all alone in the wide open spaces - apart from the 34 orcs who were fast approaching.

This fact slowly penetrated Thrugg's brain and he decided it was time to follow his friends and make a sharp exit. He turned and started a rumbling, stumbling, run for the trees. Thrugg was not built for speed. Gerald and Gertrude were watching anxiously from the trees as the man mountain began to pick up the pace. Their hearts were in their mouths as they worried about the safety of their friend.

Gertrude said half under her breath, as if to reassure herself, "He's going to make it." Gerald thought about this before replying: "Unless he stumbles and falls over."

Have you ever had one of those moments when you wished you'd never said something? Those times when it is as if by saying something you make it happen? Well, that's how Gerald felt just a couple of heartbeats later when Thrugg's left foot unerringly found the rock hidden amidst the long grass. Over he went as if he was a giant oak felled by a lumberjack with a single swing of a mighty axe. Gertrude and Gerald cringed as they felt the ground shake under the impact. They watched in horror as the orcs swarmed around the fallen body. Surely this was the end for their companion.

It was too much for Gerald. He knew he had to do something, even if it meant he was going to die as well. He started forward as he reached for the daggers in his boots, only to be restrained by Gertrude's gentle hand. He looked up, desperately, urgently, into the eyes of his healer and confidant. "Wait," she said quietly but with an authority that stopped Gerald in his tracks. "Wait?" Gerald croaked. He could barely get the word out as his voice was choked his emotion. "They'll tear him apart and my friends don't die alone!"

"Think a minute," Gertrude continued in her quiet, controlled way. "How many orcs were there?" Gerald with growing impatience snapped back; "He said there were 34!" Gertrude nodded in agreement before continuing, "And who is it that has fallen over?" "Thrugg you numbskull," came the snapped reply and Gertrude watched as Gerald listened to what he had been saying. His body relaxed and his attitude lost its urgency for action. Turning to watch the events beyond the trees, it was his time to observe something half to himself. "This will be fun," he said.

Out on the plain before them the one sided battle was unfolding. Contrary to expectation it was the orcs who were coming off worse. One by one they were flying out of the heap of the mêlée with Thrugg at its heart. Their bodies were piling up all over the heath land. It didn't take long for the fight to finish. The last remaining 4 orcs were fleeing for their lives back towards the hill they had so recently streamed down with their companions. Thrugg was left picking himself up amid the carnage he had created. His only weapon - the sack of "cabbages" - hanging loosely in his hand. Although he was covered in dust and sweat there wasn't a scratch on him.

His companions, and their reluctant guide, emerged from the trees to meet Thrugg at the edge of the woods. He seemed frustrated, almost angry, by the events that had so recently unfolded. Eldon tried to mend what he saw as the broken fences: "I'm sorry we didn't wait for you, Thrugg, but we knew you'd be alright. After all, there were only 34 of them." The mediation seemed to leave Thrugg completely unaffected. He still had a morose and petulant look on his face as he stared out into the distance at the fleeing orcs. It was too much for Eldon. He couldn't leave the matter there.

"Are you hurt?" he demanded to receive a simple shake of the head as a reply. "Well, what on earth is the matter?" came the follow up question. There followed the usual long pause before Thrugg stopped looking at the now empty distant hills and turned to face his leader. "They got away," came the answer quickly followed by "Where's he going?"

Typically Eldon responded to the first part of the statement before hearing the rest: "Well, you did alright dealing with 30 of them on your own ... Where's who going?" Thrugg stretched out his tree trunk like arm and pointed at their guide as he said "Him." Turning to look, the rest of the party became aware that the bandit was trying to make a break for it.

Quickbeam was the first to react. Scrambling for his spell book, he immediately rattled off a spell and the thug found himself restrained by lines of force at the edge of the woods. Try as he might, he was held fast and it seemed there was nothing that he could do. It took all his strength for him to mutter, "You've cheated me!"

The adventurers looked from one another to see who was going to admit to this crime. It was clear from all the blank expressions that no one had the faintest idea what he was going on about. Eldon turned to address the immobile thug: "What on earth are you talking about? It was you that led us into the heart of the orc's tribal lands." Still struggling against the restraining field the bandit spat out: "The gold!"

None the wiser the companions once more reviewed the situation. It was Gertrude, as usual, who made sense of the confusing matters. It was she who spotted the sack of "gold" that had burst open and scattered its contents amongst the bodies of the orcs. Everywhere you looked were cabbages - and not a gold coin to be seen. Their ruse had been rumbled because of Thrugg's urgent need for a brawling weapon to save his skin. As soon as this had been pointed out the argument started. Each of the adventurers was trying to blame the other four for the mistake.

Gertrude insisted she had told Eldon that Rogo would have hired them a chest if they had asked, and that would have been much more suited for the task in hand. Eldon tried to insist it was all Thrugg's fault because he could have disposed of all the orcs with his bare hands. There was no reason for him to make use of the improvised weapon and give away their secret. Quickbeam pitched in by saying if only they had given him a little more time back in Sham he could have come up with a spell that would have forced their 'guide' to give up the secret of their destination without the necessity for the deception of the sack. Gerald loftily said that he had preferred the sneaky approach all along. They should have simply said it would take time to get the cash together and then he could have followed the bandit back to their hideout.

Only Thrugg stood aloof. He was still watching their guide who was struggling to free his feet. He knew what was going to happen. Sure enough, as the argument rumbled on, Quickbeam's spell ran out and the thug was free to move once more. And move he did, making off down the narrow path through the trees. This is what Thrugg had been waiting for and he announced the news to his fellow adventurers: "He's off again."

That stopped them talking amongst themselves. As one man they turned and ran after the fleeing bandit. As they entered the woods they were able to see that he had too much of a head start. He was almost away and free. Eldon took the fateful decision. "Gerald. Stop him. Now." he ordered.

Pulling a throwing dagger from his right boot Gerald readied himself. Leg, left leg, he thought as he shaped to throw. But the action was never completed as an arrow with blue and white fletching appeared in the small of the bandit's back. Frozen in mid action, wondering how he had managed to do that, Gerald watched as the bandit fell lifeless, face down, in the dust.

Then the realisation came to him. There was another hunter in the woods and he might be the next victim. Gerald gave voice to that realisation with a shout of "Cover!" He then joined his mates as they dived and scattered into the undergrowth. Within a matter of seconds the woods appeared empty apart from the slowly cooling body lying face down in the dust. There was not a sound as if the world was holding it's breath to see what was going to happen next.

In the bushes Eldon and Quickbeam were crouched, close together. For a time they did nothing but lie still and listen. Their eyes were everywhere as they tried to assess what was happening beyond their hiding place. Despite his best efforts, this inactivity became too much for Eldon. He squirmed sideways until his mouth was next to Quickbeam's right ear. "What did you see?" he hissed.

Quickbeam, laying aside the immediate thoughts of how to deal with a wet ear and the person who caused it, considered the question word by word. This took some time. Eldon was getting furious about the delay and was about to ask again when the decision was finally made. In a slow and measured manner, designed to create the greatest amount of wetness in Eldon's ear, he hissed his reply: "An arrow with blue and white fletching came out of the bushes and struck our guide in the small of his back. It was obviously very accurately aimed and had instantly fatal effects. The good for nothing bandit fell face first into the mud. All I could think of was that there went our only hope of ever rescuing the King or of getting any treasure."

There was a pause while they both considered this further. Quickbeam continued: "And I think getting back to Sham might be a little difficult as well. Did you see who shot the arrow?" Eldon was panic stricken. Had he missed seeing one of their long last enemies come back to hunt and haunt them? Or was it simply more orcs? Desperately he hissed back: "No. Did you?" Crestfallen, Quickbeam was forced to reply that he had also failed to see their hunter.

So there they were, side by side in the dappled sunshine amongst the bushes, their heads turning this way and that, their ears straining to catch the slightest sound of anyone getting closer. They were trying not to let the tension get to them but the urge to do something - anything - was growing stronger and stronger within them.

On the other side of the track, in another clump of bushes, Gertrude was wishing she was somewhere else. She didn't have time to dive for cover under her own steam. Thrugg had been trained well by Gerald for circumstances just like this one. As soon as Gerald had said "Cov...", Thrugg had grabbed her and bundled her out of harm's away. As Gerald concluded his shout with an "...er!" Thrugg offered her greater protection by lying on top of her. And it hurt.

Gertrude couldn't take it any longer. She hissed in a voice, muffled by the sheer bulk of her protective overcoat: "Will you get off me you oaf before you squash all the life out of me!" Thrugg thought about what she had asked and began one of his logical but awfully slow replies: "Gerald has told me on many occasions that you are the most important member of the party. When the trouble starts you have to be protected so that you can put Eldon back together again when it all calms down again. He has told me that whenever he shouts 'Cover!' I'm to make sure you are not only in cover but protected from the danger that threatens."

Along with his weight, this ponderous answer was almost too much for Gertrude. Somehow though she managed to control her temper and met steamroller logic with the more active form of her own. "Thrugg," she asked, "can you see any sign of danger threatening us at present." There was a pause and Gertrude felt Thrugg making a slow, careful, survey of their immediate surroundings. There was another pause and Gertrude knew that her protective blanket - no, mattress more like - was taking the time to listen very carefully as he had been trained. Finally he reached his conclusion: "I can sense no immediate danger," he said.

Gertrude decided that it was time for drastic measure. She used the most imperative of her voices that even in the whisper produced immediate results: "Then get off me NOW!" she hissed. Thrugg rolled to her side. Despite his best efforts it still sounded like another tree falling in the forest but at least Gertrude could move and breath again.

Once she had recovered from Thrugg's attempts to turn her into a pressed flower she conducted her own assessment of the situation. She looked, listened and made use of her special skills to reach out amongst the bushes to find out what was what. After a few moments she was forced to the same conclusion and told Thrugg: "You're right as far as I can tell. I can sense no immediate danger either."

It all goes to show that even finely hewn adventuring skills are sometimes not enough. Not twenty feet away from where this couple lay, the person who had fired the arrow crouched. Clad in mottled green and brown he held his long bow with an easy confidence in his hands. Already another arrow was notched. He was pointing it towards the bushes where Gertrude and Thrugg were, even though there was no tension in the bowstring. He was watching, listening, waiting with the assured skills of an accomplished hunter. His patience was rewarded for once more a whispered conversation was in progress.

A thought had completed the somewhat lengthy journey required to pop into Thrugg's head. Nervously he started scanned the bushes about him. Gertrude sensed his movements and turned her head away from scanning her part of the forest to see what was up. She didn't like what she saw. Thrugg was definitely worried and that meant they could be in real trouble. Gently she reached out a hand and placed it on his arm. He nearly leapt out of his skin.

He turned to look at Gertrude and their eyes met. He understood her look - she'd used it before when she wanted to ask him what he was thinking. he moistened his lips before making another frantic search of the area with his eyes. Then, once more locking gazes, he gave his fears voice: "I hope it's not goblins. You know how I can't stand goblins!" Gertrude closed her eyes with the frustration. She thought to herself:

"You won't stand me after I've finished with you either!". But kinder thoughts took over and she felt she at least had to humour her companion.

In her gentlest of voices she asked: "Have you seen anything to make you think it might be goblins?" Thrugg thought for a moment - well, nearly a minute in fact - before shaking his head. Gertrude knew she'd got his full attention now so she pressed on: "What about the arrow? What does that tell you?" She watched Thrugg's face and knew that he was repaying every moment of the arrows flight into the bandit's back.

Finally the replay was over and Thrugg could give his considered opinion: "It was a long bow arrow. Goblins never use long bows. So it not goblins. More likely another bandit." Gertrude nodded in agreement and concluded "Very likely a case of dog eat dog." They both resumed the scanning of the bushes around them hoping to catch some sign of what they thought would be just another bandit.

But, as we know, it was a highly skilled woodsman who was hunting down his prey in this particular stretch of woodland. He had waited for the whispered conversation to make his move. Their voices would cover louder sounds than the scout might make on his passage through the bushes. While they talked, he took the opportunity to close in on his prey. Now he was only feet away from Gertrude and Thrugg and waiting to make his entrance.

When Thrugg had his back to him the hunter slid out of the bushes. Gertrude was looking straight ahead so missed the entrance as well. Thrugg turned back and saw him first. Thrugg froze in horror as now the bow was drawn with an arrow pointing straight at Gertrude's back. Thrugg didn't know what to do and reached out to Gertrude to seek her help. Misinterpreting the contact from Thrugg, Gertrude offered further reassurance: "And before you ask, I don't think it's more orcs either. It much too soon for the ones that got away to have got some of their mates to come back. As I said, just another bandit. We'll just lie here, keep quiet and see what develops."

The hunter decided it was time to join in with this conversation. He hissed in a voice that could not be heard beyond the bush under which three of them now crouched: "That's a very good idea. Let's all lie still, keep quiet and see what develops - and then this little lady doesn't get my arrow in her back." Gertrude broiled at the 'little lady' jibe but in the circumstances decided she would just have to swallow her pride - for now.

So there they all lay, quietly in the dappled sunshine, waiting to see what happened next.

As you might expect it fell to Eldon to break the stillness that had descended on this part of the woodland. Under his bush he turned once more to Quickbeam to explain his proposed course of action. "It's too quiet," he said. "I've got to find out if the rest are alright." Quickbeam replied "And how do you propose to do that?" and knew that he had just precipitated disaster. "Like this," Eldon hissed before shouting at the top of his voice: "Thrugg!"

The few birds that had plucked up courage to sneak back to the local trees took off again in a flurry of feathers and leaves. But no other sound was heard by Eldon or his wizard companion. In fact, Thrugg had drawn breath to shout a reply when the hunter had stopped him with a shake of his head. The movement he made with his bow was a clear sign that if he made any noise Gertrude got an arrow in her back. Even Thrugg could understand that sort of message and he remained silent.

That didn't go down too well under Eldon and Quickbeam's bush. It increased Eldon's concern and, before Quickbeam could offer any counsel, let alone stop him, he called again: "Gertrude!!" Once more silence was the only answer. Now Eldon was really worried. Turning to his friend he anxiously blurted out: "Quickbeam. There's no one out there. They're all dead. We're the only ones left!"

"Not for long if you go on like this," thought the wizard to himself. Out loud he provided Eldon with a life line: "Aren't you forgetting someone?" It took Eldon a while but he got there in the end. "Gerald!!!" he bellowed in his best parade ground shout. There followed a pause that while it only lasted less than a minute seemed like an eternity to Eldon. Finally his shouts were about to receive a reply.

From another nearby clump of bushes Gerald responded with a shout of his own: "Yeah? What do you want?" Quickbeam watched as Eldon visibly relax upon learning that they weren't the only two left of their party. Eldon soon brightened up now and became the pompous leader they all knew and love. "Get yourself over here with us two this instant!" he barked towards the unseen Gerald. "I can't for a minute," came the reply by return.

Quickbeam thought that Eldon was going to have a seizure. Fancy a mere scout disobeying the orders of the recognised leader and brains of their group! Quickbeam smiled to himself as he watched this reaction from Eldon. It took Eldon several moments to overcome the rebuff and bark out: "What is it that you're doing that so damn important?"

"I'm lying in these bushes," began the saga, "along with Gertrude, Thrugg and the bloke who just shot our guide. He's thinking about putting an arrow into Gertrude but has just become aware of my dagger resting in the small of his back." There was a short pause as everyone in earshot took in this change in their situations. Gerald continued his running commentary: "Ah! He's got the idea that sudden moves would be a mistake and is slowly letting the tension out of the bowstring. Now he's laying the bow on the ground and we're all going to come slowly to our feet. Why don't you two come over and join us?"

The six figures slowly rose out of their two clumps of bushes. Some of them were obviously quite pleased with the outcome. Eldon was grinning like the cat that had got the cream - which, when you consider all he'd done was to lie in some bushes and shout a lot, was a little arrogant of him. Thrugg was trying to make amends for his earlier pancake landing by helping Gertrude to her feet, only to receive a bruised shin for his trouble. She always had a good left boot, Quickbeam thought to himself as he adjusted the fall of his robes.

Gerald had the usual casual but alert look in his eyes. He was watching every move of the newcomer to their group. This was the one person to have risen out of the bushes who was not happy, definitely not happy. He knew he had been defeated by a superior hunter and was worried what that was going to mean to his immediate future. The sight of Eldon striding towards him in triumph, making enough noise to be heard in the next county but having fully regained the initiative, only served to deepen his gloom.

Looking at this newcomer an outsider would have instantly recognised him as a professional hunter of some sort. He was clad in a mixture of brown, green and grey that meant it was hard to see him against the woodland background even when he was standing in plain sight. Despite having been trapped, you could sense the pent up animal instincts within him. His brown eyes set in a suntanned, weather beaten face were never still. At first glance it might have seemed like he was seeking an escape route but that was not the case. Another hunter would recognise that he was constantly updating his information of the world around him. The hunter always seeking prey, always assessing the dangers.

Gerald stood directly behind him. From his point of view the set of the shoulders told it all. Even though it looked like recent events had left him untouched, the hunter had resigned himself to the fact that this encounter was only going to end one way. The hunter had become the hunted and was about to become the prey - the dead prey. Gerald sensed that there was one desperate throw of the dice left in this bowman in the woods. The dagger was ready to bring that action to an end before anyone else got hurt.

Eldon strode towards the small group with his usual air of command. "Right my good and loyal friends, what are we going to do with this bandit? He is clearly a murderer having killed our guide so I guess we string him up to the nearest tree as a lesson to others." The self appointed judge and jury paused before continuing: "Thrugg. Get a rope." Thrugg began to rummage in his back pack. Gerald saw a stiffening of the hunter's muscles and lay a reassuring rather than threatening hand on the shoulder before him. The hunter got the message and relaxed.

Gertrude spoke for them all: "Eldon, you can't do that." This generated more bluster in the group's apparent leader: "Why not? Rogo appointed me magistrate of Sham and as such I am the law. I can hang murderers, you know." Gertrude replied in her usual child educating voice: "Yes, I know. But look at him and tell me what you see." This confused Eldon who looked from Gertrude to hunter, then into Gerald's eyes which told him nothing, before settling onto the condemned man again.

No matter how hard he tried, enlightenment would not come. Eldon could not discern the subtle clue that had caught Gertrude's eye. Eldon knew he was going to have to pretend that he had seen whatever it was he couldn't. Confidently he addressed his friend: "Of course I saw that. Let's get him strung up and get it over with. It makes no difference." Gertrude's voice dripped with sarcasm: "And after we've strung up a Ducal Ranger, what do you suggest we do then? Become outlaws and robbers or turn ourselves over to Zama for her gentle attentions?"

There was a moment as Eldon, Quickbeam and Thrugg all took in what Gertrude had said. From his expression it was clear that Gerald was a party to this secret. Slowly one by one the others made a more careful examination of the hunter who stood before them. There it was. On his left breast, almost invisible amongst the camouflage despite it's silver colour. The symbol was that of an officer in the service of the Duke. He was their equal, if not their superior, in the war of the lawful against the unlawful. And Eldon had ordered his summary execution. There was a pause while this was slowly taken in.

Thrugg was the first to voice his conclusion to the whole matter. "I don't want to do anything that might upset Zama," he said with a heavy heart. There was yet another pause while everyone who knew Zama thought about what she would do if she found out they'd even thought about stringing up a Duke's officer. From the expressions on their faces you could tell they were not pleasant thoughts they were having. Gerald and his new found friend the Ranger looked from face to face, reading the fear in the eyes of the other adventurers. Finally Gerald shrugged his shoulders and the Ranger understood.

"Look," he said, breaking the silence, "No harm done. We all make mistakes from time to time." Eldon bristled at this and began to repudiate this statement: "How dare you! I never ... ow!" This statement was cut short as Gertrude delivered a sharp kick to his ankle. She, at least, was determined that matters were not going to get any worse. "What he means," she said, "Is that he never dreamt of saying that you had made any mistakes. If there was any misunderstanding in this situation the fault was all ours." She ended her statement with yet another glare at her leader.

"Yes. Sorry," Eldon finally muttered. Gerald pitched into the troubled waters smoothing by adding: "And I trust you won't take my sneaking up on you as too much of an offence. I was just lucky." The Ranger looked Gerald straight in the eyes: "I'd heard of you before I came into these parts. They said you were good. But I never imagined that you would be that good." There was a moment as the two highly skilled scouts acknowledged the bond of their craft. "I'm Gerald," he said. "Hector of Candorum," came the reply and an offered hand. Gerald took it and, while the others thought it was a simple expression of friendship, exchanged the expected secret signal with his new found ally.

Gertrude felt she had to step in before she was sick. All this gooey stuff just didn't fit well with the image she had of her friend. "Enough of this," she said, "What about him?" Everyone turned to look where she was pointing. The body of their one time guide still lay face down in the dust with Hector's arrow in his back. "I'd forgotten about him," Eldon observed to himself. "I don't think he'll mind, " Thrugg added with his usual extraordinary insight.

"I know that," Eldon continued, "But how on earth are we going to find the King now?" "King?" asked the Ranger which provoked a discussion about how this group of adventurers came to be passing through Hector's patrol area.

As the conversation unfolded it became clear that the Ranger had been watching the bandit group, of which the ex-guide was once a member, for some time. It seemed that they had been systematically fleecing the area to the east of Sham and had only recently turned their attentions in the direction of that village. This group had been wanted for some time by the authorities after committing all sorts of crimes. Hector was just biding his time until reinforcements arrived so that they could attack the bandits' hideout.

He was surprised to see the heroes in the company of the bandit. Assuming that they had been tricked in some way he had killed the guide in order to rescue them from their dilemma. The Ranger was somewhat surprised to hear of the King of Battenburgh's involvement with the adventurer's side of the story.

And that's when the next argument started. Hector wanted to claim jurisdiction - and the rewards that would come with the removal of this threat to law and order in Chouse. The heroes insisted that it was their duty to rescue the King and any rewards that might arise from such a mission would rightfully be theirs. It took some time for this dispute to be settled.

In the end the heroes from Sham had to give way. After all only the Ranger knew where the bandits' hideout was. Without that information there was nothing Eldon and his band could do to complete their mission. Despite the back and forth it all came down to money in the end. The compromise that was reached granted to the Ranger all rewards from the destruction of the outlaw band while rewarding the heroes with any treasure they could find within the hideout - and any reward they could extract from the rescued King.

Despite the complexity of the negotiations it didn't take that long. The body on the path was barely cold before the band was once more moving through the woods. This time however you would have had to look hard to mark their passage. This group was now in hunter mode. Led by Gerald and their new found companion, the rest of them passed like shadows amongst the dappled shade under the trees. Nothing was going to surprise them now. And it was not long before they reached their destination.

Rising out of the sea of trees was a stone bluff known as Lover's Leap. It was here that legend said a dwarven warrior and his elven love had chosen to join in a mutual death pact rather than submit to the will of their respective tribes. Such was the animosity between the races that even true love could not overcome it.

Crouching in the bushes with the Ranger alongside him, Gerald recalled how it had only been the previous evening back in Sham when Rogo had told this very tale. The inn had seen some visitors that evening. Just a small band of elves passing through on their way to Seaport but enough to ruffle the feathers of the regulars from the castle who had managed to save a few beans for the eve of pay day preparatory flagon or five. Zama had sensed trouble and told Rogo to tell a tale to calm things down.

Shame it didn't have the desired effect. Long before he'd got to the good bit where the two lovers swore to be faithful to the end. Ages before he'd described how their protestations of mutual adoration had been rejected by both their tribal councils. And way before the part that always brought tears to even Gerald's hardened eyes when they took the fateful decision on the edge of this very cliff by the light of the full moon all sorts of mayhem had already broken out in the inn.

Even now Gerald wasn't quite sure who'd thrown the first stool. The dwarves had tried to rile the visitors with their usual chant of 'Pointys go home' but the elves had offered no reaction to that. Expressions of that sort of prejudice just showed a complete lack of understanding. Gerald recalled the very clever counter move when the elves started to try and find any reason for dwarven existence - and as usual could come up with none. By now the more cautious locals had left for an early night and Gerald, along with the other interested spectators, had taken up a defensive position in one of the safer corners.

Then the two groups started to trade insults. Again this was according to established practice. That went really well. Gerald remembered applauding some of the choicer ripostes - and from both sides as well. But it was never going to end in any other way than a fight. But that was fun to watch too. As was the 'discussion' between Zama and Rogo when she reminded him that next time he should tell the story about how Jack killed seven with one blow. That didn't have dwarves or elves in it - only trolls and flies - and they never came into the Portly Pixie to settle their racial differences.

Gerald remembered being very careful not to applaud that - after all they were both his friends.

So, last night it was the story about Lover's Leap and today it's the place itself. Once more Gerald looked up at the sheer sided cliff before him. He tried to picture an elf and dwarf throwing themselves off the top, hand in hand, to certain death. There was no way could he picture it. The only answer he could come up with was that the dwarf pushed the elf and over balanced afterwards. Another idle thought crossed his mind. Maybe he should get Magistrate Eldon to investigate the story on the pretext of one tribe demanding reparations from the other. That'd pass an interesting hour or two!

He was stirred from these musings by the slightest of pressures on his arm. Hector was pointing at a small cleft at the base of the cliff. "Well," Gerald thought to himself, "At least I've not got to persuade Thrugg to climb the damn thing!" He squinted as he looked more closely at the deeper patch of the darkness amid the shadows. Finally, with the slightest of nods, he offered his agreement and the two scouts made their silent and shadowy way back to where the rest of the band were waiting.

As usual Eldon was as impatient as ever. "Well?" he demanded as soon as he saw Gerald - which was some 30 seconds or more after he had actually arrived before him. "We're agreed," came the reply supported by a nod from the Ranger. "An entrance to the bandit's hideout is through one of the openings known locally as Lover's Death. If we want to rescue the King that's the way we need to go. Carefully and quietly." There was a moment while Eldon wondered if Gerald was trying to make some personal point. In the end he concluded that he was being over sensitive and nodded his agreement to the plan.

"We've got a deal then?" the Ranger asked. "We have a deal," Eldon replied. "We'll go in and rescue the King while you go and gather your forces. You'll be back at dawn tomorrow when you can clean out the rest of the bandits to claim your rewards. We'll keep the treasure we find." The Ranger gave a half nod to confirm his acceptance of the terms and suddenly wasn't there anymore. Even Gerald was amazed by the Hector's ability to blend into the forest background and made a mental note to have a professional discussion with him once this little escapade was over.

The heroes checked their equipment and prepared themselves. It was just another short walk through the woods that took them to the rocks. Eldon and the others then stood by the cleft in the rocks. It was obviously an opening that led deep into the hillside. There was no sound or movement anywhere close to this opening. Now that the Ranger had melted away into the trees, all that was left for the adventurers was to go forward into the shadows before them.

Even Eldon's eyes could see that there had been a lot of traffic in and out of the darkness that lay beyond. Many feet had left their prints in the muddy ground. As leader he knew it fell to him to devise a plan. He raised his eyes and looked into the cleft itself. He stared hard, as if he was hoping that the harder he looked the more he could see. In fact the harder he looked, the more his head hurt. He knew that they were going to have to go into the darkness to see what lay behind. It was just that he wasn't quite ready yet. Perhaps something would happen to help him make up his mind.

Strangely enough his wish did come true. Gertrude, standing just behind him, hissed into his ear and he felt like he jumped a mile into the air with the shock. Pulling himself together he reflected on what she had said: "What are you waiting for? Why not just do what we always do?" It took a further moment for him to still his shaking heart and gather his scrambled thoughts. Finally he remember what they always did in these circumstances. He turned to his companions crouched, ready for action, in a small group behind him.

"Gerald," he instructed, "Off you go and see what you can find." The party's chief scout and all round sneaky person nodded his acceptance of the order. Catlike he made his way past his fellows and entered the shades that hid who knew what.

Chapter 6: Into the Dark

Gerald only went a few paces into the rock lined tunnel that lay beyond the entrance before he stopped. Leaning carefully against the wall he became motionless. He stilled his breathing and tried to become one with the rock that was behind him and the darkness around him. Experience had taught him that once he was out of the light it was a good idea to take a few minutes to let his eyes get used to what at first seemed the pitch dark. So he stood, silent and still, listening with all his senses to the world around him.

Sure enough the longer he stood, the more was revealed to him. He could hear his friends waiting at the entrance behind him. Even though they were highly skilled adventurers and waited in silence for their scout to report, they were still making noise. Gerald could hear Thrugg breathing - he always sounded like a wild boar even to the untrained ear. From the sound of the turning pages Gerald knew Quickbeam was checking his spells, getting ready for anything. The sounds of small stones being moved told the scout that Eldon was impatient and just couldn't keep his feet still. Only Gertrude remained undetected by her friend. That gave him small measure of comfort. Gerald knew that she, at least, had turned all her attention towards the dark cleft and his actions beyond.

At last he knew he had stood still long enough. His eyes had switched over to night vision and he could see where he was going, to some extent. Avoiding looking backwards at the opening where the light now seemed to stream in with blinding exuberance, he looked down the corridor-like cave. There was nothing to see beyond the walls worn smooth by the passage of water years ago and a few scattered stones on the floor. No sound reached his straining ears. There was no more to be learnt from the darkness beyond by staying still. It was time to move.

Like one more shadow amongst the rest, Gerald began to slide further into the darkness. This was his territory. This was his workplace. This was where he excelled. And it wasn't long before he was faced with another decision. The passageway split and he had to choose one of two ways to go forward.

Gerald used all his senses to assess the best route to take. He looked down each way forward, only to be forced to accept that each was equally dark. He listened carefully and the only sounds he could detect were those faint and now far distant noises of his waiting friends at the entrance. He even used his nose but each way forward seemed to emit the same foul odour. There seemed to be no difference between them. They were equally unattractive and he was going to have to make a difficult choice.

Crouching in the darkness, he reviewed the situation. He thought to himself: "Eldon always says when faced with a choice be sure to make the right one." The darkness hid his grin as he whispered to himself: "Left it is then!" and he started down the left hand passageway.

Afterwards Gerald put it down to being too concerned about what might be in front of him as the reason that he overlooked what was directly underneath his feet. He hadn't gone more than 3 paces along his chosen route before he felt something move beneath his foot. Instantly he drew a knife and flattened himself against one of the walls. But it was already too late.

Just behind him there was a rumbling and a scraping. Dust was falling from the ceiling. From a slot, unseen until now, a portcullis was falling to seal off any hope of escape. While the iron from which it was made appeared wet and rusty, the thump it made as it hit the floor spoke of the strength of its construction. Once that sound had passed, swallowed up by the all enfolding darkness, Gerald could sense nothing more. It seemed to be a simple rat trap, and he was the trapped rat. "Guess Eldon would have been right this time," was the thought that crossed his mind as he waited for whatever was going to happen next.

At the entrance the sound of the falling portcullis did not pass unnoticed. Faint as it was it was still loud enough to attract Thrugg's attention away from studying the woods about them and Quickbeam from his book. Eldon heard it and was immediately apprehensive. He was going to have to come up with a plan and he didn't know what was going to be best to do. Luckily Gertrude once more saved his day.

"Move," she instructed as she led the way into the darkness. The rest of the party followed, spells and weapons at the ready, Eldon for once at the rear, overtaken by his fellow adventurers' desperate rush to aid their friend. In less than a minute they covered the distance that had taken Gerald more than a quarter of an hour to cross. Thrugg was the first to discover the portcullis - by simply running into it. That brought the rest to a slithering, skidding, stop in the darkness. Gerald spoke to his friend from the other side of the trap: "Well made, isn't Thrugg?" he asked. "Yes," came the nasal reply, "It hurt my nose." "Well, see if you can lift it and I can kiss it better for you," Gerald suggested out of the darkness.

Thrugg, reflecting to himself that he'd rather have Gertrude put him back together than let Gerald kiss him, bent to his allotted task. Gripping the bars tightly he applied all of his strength to force the confining grill back into the ceiling slot from which it had fallen. But it was no use. It resisted even his great strength. It was not going to move. Even when he bent his knees and added the not inconsiderable force of his legs to that of his arms Gerald was going to be firmly trapped in his rat trap.

Admitting defeat, and feeling the fatigue in his limbs Thrugg finally sank to his knees amongst the slime.

"I guess I'm going to have to find how to unlock it from my side - or see what waits in the darkness beyond," Gerald observed with a resigned tone to his voice. "At least the other way seemed clear so off you lot go and I'll see you later." It fell to Gertrude to disprove her friend's assertion. She had been guarding that opening, straining all her senses to be prepared for anything coming at them out of the darkness. Now she brought her friends up to date with the latest observations. "It may have been clear before that portcullis fell, but for the last two or three minutes I've been hearing scuffling and snuffling noises." That brought an immediate silence and stillness amongst her friends as they all turned their attentions towards the right hand tunnel.

Sure enough, something was definitely moving about down there now. It sounded like a creature of some sort. The adventurers' minds were racing through a checklist of tunnel dwelling creatures they had encountered in the past and each of them was preparing the necessary defensive action. After another few tension filled minutes, Gertrude spoke again: "It doesn't seem to be coming any closer. Maybe Gerald just woke something with his carelessness," she said.

"Maybe it can't come any closer. Someone will have to go and look," observed Quickbeam. He knew as soon as he said it he'd made a mistake. Eldon's next comment confirmed his worse fears: "Thank you, Quickbeam." Three little words that made Quickbeam's mood sag further than his shoulders did. Now he had been promoted to Chief Scout amongst the far from happy band. But he knew that there was no use arguing. He was going to have to go and see what was making the noises on behalf of the rest of them. Cursing his own big mouth, gripping his spell book and tightening the belt that restrained his robes he started into the pitch dark of the right hand tunnel that Gerald had rejected.

That tunnel curved slightly to the left as the wizard made his cautious way forward. The further he went the clearer the noises in front of him became. There was definitely something big just around the next corner. Quickbeam stopped and began to worry about what he could do. Looking back into the darkness where he had left his friends he realized that he could hardly hear them. He felt very much alone. He looked forward once more and became aware that there was a light at the end of this particular tunnel. Flickering, dim, yellow light seemed to wait just around the seemingly never ending corner.

In the dank darkness Quickbeam thought to himself: "Eldon said forward and at least there's some light in that direction. So forward I go." He began again his slow progress along the wall of the tunnel in the cave. As the light grew brighter, his confidence returned. Now at least he could see his spell book and he slid it into his hand, ready for action. He was almost round the corner now and could see what lay in front.

The light was coming from a torch that had been pushed into a mounting on the wall. It burned with a smoky yellow flame whose light was soon swallowed by the deep surrounding darkness. But it gave enough illumination for Quickbeam to see what was making the snuffling and snarling noises. And he didn't like what he saw. Frozen against the wall Quickbeam absorbed the changed circumstances of his situation.

The creature he was looking at stood about the same height as a man, but that's where all resemblance ended. It was covered with grayish brown fur that seemed to have a slimy sheen of its own. Arms and legs were similarly covered and ended in wicked claws. They were curved and yellow, although stained with a dark residue which could only be dried blood. This is how the creature tore its prey apart. The head was no better. A long muzzle ending in a black snout on top of a jaw full of the cruelest teeth ever seen confirmed the nature of the beast. It's was clearly a large dog-like being - and the sheen on the fur identified it to an experienced adventurer like Quickbeam as an Acid Dog.

These creatures were scavengers often found in the deep dark places of this realm. They would wait until something tasty happened by before pouncing on it. Then, either with claws or teeth, they would tear out the life of their prey before devouring it. Dangerous hunters if you were not aware they were about.

They were also well adapted to defense. The sheen on their fur was a strong acid they excreted naturally. If struck with metal weapons – commonly carried by most adventurers – the weapon was corroded in an instant. Often this would leave the attacker defenseless. Their last memory would be of a painful death in a slime filled acidic embrace full of teeth and claws.

"Good job Gerald sprung that trap," Quickbeam thought to himself, "Because the noise, along with that torch, has disturbed it. Now I know it's there, and it doesn't know about me!" And that was a good thing. Because the Acid Dog had another peculiar defense mechanism when attacked. They actually spat balls of acid at any threat. If it was to hit the target in the face the eyes would be burnt out in seconds. Then it was easy for the dog to close in and finish off the attacker. Knowing that, and wanting to keep his sight for a while longer, made Quickbeam cautious - very cautious - very, very cautious.

With one eye on the dog he began to scan the spells in his book making ready for the attack. 'Feather Fall' was the first. "Very useful if falling off a cliff but not much good in this situation," Quickbeam observed to himself and turned the page.

68

Similarly he dismissed 'Detect Magic', 'Dancing Lights' and 'Magical Fire Creation' - before finding exactly what he had been looking for. He had stopped on 'Sands of Sleep'. A ranged attack that sent the target into an instant deep sleep from which they could not be woken for several minutes. That would do nicely. He scanned the page to refresh his memory over the material components he needed to cast the spell. Silently, swiftly he assembled them from the various pockets and pouches he had for just this purpose. Clearing his mind of all distractions while focusing his energies onto the target before him, he made ready to cast the spell.

Quickbeam felt the magical energy gather about him in response to the summoning phrase he have formed in his mind. Raising the necessary bits and pieces in his right hand he began to cast the spell with the quiet authority in his voice that befitted a mage of his stature:

> Sand of time from day to night,
> Rid me of this current plight.
> While onwards I silent creep,
> Let the target fall into deep sleep.

Quickbeam completed the spell by tossing the necessary material component - a handful of sand - towards the creature. The Acid Dog who was the target of the spell had heard Quickbeam complete the spell verbally. It had even turned towards him and made ready to cover him in acid filled slime. Even though it had moved with lightening speed, the mage had been quicker. The enchanted sands of sleep hit the dog full in the face before the acid slime could be released. This came as an immense surprise to the dog. But before it could do anything more than blink, the spell took its effect and the dog reacted by falling fast asleep. Quickbeam watched as the creature slowly crumbled to the floor breathing deeply. "This scouting business is easy," thought Quickbeam as he moved into the torch lit chamber.

Wary of even this sleeping beast, Quickbeam knew his work was not yet over. As he moved into the room he knew the job had only been half done by the magic. Now it was time for the close up kill. Drawing a dagger the mage moved into the room to cut the throat of the sleeping creature. Speaking completely unnecessary and totally incongruous words of comfort and encouragement the wizard closed in on the "Nice doggy. Sleepy doggy." It was the act of a moment to slit the acid dog's throat and turn the magical sleep of a few minutes into the long sleep of death. Quickbeam relaxed as the beast breathed its last and wiped the dagger on his robes in preparation for returning it into his belt. Quickbeam was quite pleased with himself. That was no trouble at all. The deed was done and the room secured. He wondered why Gerald made this sort of thing seem so difficult. He began to look around the area that he had secured as he drew the first deep breath in ages to summon his friends.

That breath froze in his throat. He found himself looking straight into the teeth filled jaws of another acid dog less than a hand's breath from his face. Somehow, even in the midst of the abject terror that was now filling it, his mind was still working. Quickbeam was able to take in the generally brown coloration of this one, which meant this was the female. He realised that he'd probably just killed her mate while she lurked in shadows waiting for the chance to pounce. She's watched everything that he'd done and now wanted revenge. She also probably wanted Quickbeam for her tea as well.

All this took less than a second. At last the wizard was able to utter the summons for his mates. It wasn't the call he had prepared to make, but it was one that was well known amongst adventurers. With what he thought was going to be his final breath he screamed "Help!" before falling to the floor under the brown skinned rug that had teeth - and claws - and acid! After that, there was nothing else for him to do but to fight as if his very life depended on it - as it did.

Clearly a vicious, acid spitting, beast with sharp teeth and cruel claws should have been no match for a competent mage. But this mage was not competent at the moment and it looked like he is going to lose the fight. Not only had the dog's leap knocked the dagger from his hand but the jarring bump with which they had both hit the floor had driven every thought of spells from Quickbeam's mind. It was hand to fur combat and ignore the burning sensation every time you touched the dog if you wanted to stay alive. Quickbeam wanted that very much but it looked like he was going to lose. The dog had finally managed to pinion him to the floor with his front paws on Quickbeam's shoulders. All that was left was for the dog to lower his head and rip out the throat of he who had dared to kill her mate.

All that stopped this happening was the strength in Quickbeam's arms that were holding his hands around the dog's throat. But his arms were not that strong and the strength was waning. Slowly, inevitably, the head was coming down - closer and closer to their target. The sharp teeth were about to close on the soft white throat of the mage when, all of a sudden, out of nowhere, an almost black clad arm appeared around the dog's throat. Someone was trying to help Quickbeam. While the teeth were still there, straining for the life ending bite, they had halted in mid chomp. Quickbeam managed to writhe a little beneath the unwelcome overcoat. He caught a glimpse of his rescuer and could not believe his eye. It was Gerald. "How could he be here?" came the unbidden thought as they both wrestled in the slime and acid in a desperate attempt to save a wizard's life.

As it was the dog like creature was stronger than both of them. No matter how hard they tried, the dog was able to gain the upper paw. It was not long before they were back into the same position again. Quickbeam was pinned to the ground with a paw on each of his shoulders. Gerald was straddling the beast with both arms around its neck. The teeth were back moving inexorably towards Quickbeam's throat. The eyes of the two adventuring friends met and they knew that their strength was spent. This was going to be the end for one of them at least. A thought formed in Quickbeam's mind. He even felt it was going to be his final thought: "And I'll never know where in blazes Gerald came from to risk his life to save mine!" He closed his eyes in surrender to the inevitable and composed himself for death.

There was a loud roaring in his ears, as if all the beasts he'd ever slayed had come to form an honor guard in Limbo and welcome his spirit. The weight was suddenly lifted off his body. He could no longer feel the putrid breath on his face. He knew his life was spent and prepared to open his spirit's eyes to see what awaited him. Only what he heard next stopped him. He could swear that he had heard Gerald speak. Had the acid dog got him as well? Were they to be companions on the journey to the Afterlife as they had been companions in this world?

He thought back over the last few seconds and analysed what he had actually heard: "Thanks Thrugg. Is Gertrude with you?" Had the entire party been slain by this one denizen of the dark? That didn't seem possible so he fell back on the alternative explanation. Still with his eyes closed he used his whole body to feel where he was. The slime and muck on his clothes was just as it had been - and the solid stone beneath his back was still there. Nothing had changed. Even that annoying little rock easily ignored in the midst of the frenetic combat still nestled in the small of his back. So he hadn't gone anywhere. So he wasn't dead. Which meant ...

Quickbeam opened his eyes to confirm what his logical mind had already told him. There was Gerald, slumped against one of the cave walls, catching his breath after their struggle. There was the acid dog, lying in two halves, lifeless and very, very dead. There was Thrugg, obviously the reason for the bisection of the creature, wiping his sword on the oiled cloth he always carried for that very purpose. Acid dog's acid will soon pit any blade if you're not careful.

Gingerly he turned his head and saw, emerging from the tunnel, he had followed Eldon with Gertrude hurrying to reach him. Her first aid kit was already open and it wasn't long before the healing slave was being applied to the open wounds on Quickbeam's arms where the dog had almost had him. So, there they were all back together again, the bold, brave, adventurers.

As the newly discovered pain in Quickbeam's arms began to fade under Gertrude's ministrations, he felt that some gesture towards his saviours was in order. He looked from Gerald to Thrugg and could sense their relief that their friend had not become supper for the beast. He decided that the last thing they wanted was thanks but he had to say something. "Thrugg," he finally decided on, "What kept you? I thought you were always ready to back up the scout when he was in trouble?" Quickbeam saw that he'd got that just right. Thrugg was agonising over not getting there sooner and the telling off from Quickbeam enabled him to acknowledge his failing. His oversized boots stirred the grime on the cavern floor as he lowered his head in penitent submission. Quickbeam turned his mock anger gratitude onto Gerald: "And I don't know what you were playing at! Pretending to be trapped so that you could make this grandstand gesture of rescuing the helpless mage - and that nearly got both of us killed!"

Gerald let this sink in as he rose slowly to his feet. In the end he had formulated the answer. He crossed to Quickbeam and roughly hauled him upright. Gerald pushed something into Quickbeam's hand. Looking down the wizard saw that it was his spell book that had gone flying in the first desperate lunge from the acid dog. "Next time," Gerald said, not unkindly, "watch your own damn backs. I might not be able to find a way to help you on that occasion. As it is I think I've stirred up more trouble for us all."

This statement brought the party back into their usual state of instant readiness. With a nod of the head Gerald indicated the second tunnel that led from the acid dogs' lair. Quickbeam and the others suddenly realised that it was from this that the scout had arrived to aid his friend. Following Gerald's lead they began to move cautiously along that new pathway under the ground. They had not gone very far when the tunnel split. Gerald pointed up the left hand branch. "Portcullis" he whispered and they all turned their attention to the other tunnel. There it was very plain to see the trouble that the scout's urgent rescue mission had stirred up for them all.

This new passage was rock lined and narrow like the one that led to the trap that had hindered Gerald's forward progress. But within a few paces it was clear that this was another way forward. It was opening out and in the middle distance a lantern was burning so that the extent of the larger chamber could be clearly seen. The heroes crouched in the last vestiges of the shadows as they surveyed the scene before them.

It was certainly a large chamber. Not only did the roof soar to dimly seen heights but the floor fell to greater depths. It was as if some giant axe blade wielded by the gods had struck this section of their underground world. The only way forward lay across a slender rock arch that formed a bridge over the gulf. It was at the far end of that bridge that the lantern burnt. And by it stood a guard.

It was obvious that the noise of the portcullis and the fight with the acid dogs had placed him on alert. He stood, sword in hand, warily looking across the bridge towards the shadows in which the heroes crouched. He was straining to catch sight or sound of whatever it was that was coming his way. The constant moistening of his lips showed he was nervous but, as the true professional thug he was, he was going to stand his ground. After all, whatever or whoever it was could only come at him one at a time over the narrow rock bridge. It would be a simple job to sweep them aside and into the unseen depths with his sword.

Once they all had had a chance to take in the scene, Gerald made a slight motion with his hand. The small group silently made their way back to the chamber where the bodies of the Acid Dogs were cooling and slowly dissolving in their own body fluids. There a whispered conversation was held. At first Eldon insisted as the leader of the group he should go first and simply remove the brigand with his fencing skills. The others knew a disaster in the making and it fell to Gertrude to use all her persuasive charm to get him to see sense. As Quickbeam was still recovering from his unfortunate brush with the monsters that now lay at his feet, she agreed that it was going to take frontal attack to overcome this latest obstacle. However, she went on, surely he could see that the foe who bared their route was not worthy of his attentions. He was only a simple bandit and Eldon should save his energies for a more worthy opponent - such as the leader of this band.

Surely Eldon would agree with her that this current task was much more suited to one of his followers - Thrugg for example. The others were quick to agree - because they knew that Thrugg had the better head for heights and was less likely to fall off the bridge. And so it was settled. Eldon's plan for a straight on, heads forward, approach was approved but it would be Thrugg who was to lead the way.

A few moments later the guard at the bridge stiffened in fear and went white at the sight of the man mountain that was Thrugg striding out of the shadows at the other end of the bridge. It took him a few seconds to remember his orders. Thrugg was already on the bridge when the guard barked out: "Halt and give the password!" Unfortunately most of the sound got caught up somewhere in the back of his throat and what came out was more like a croak than a bellow. Strangely though it had the desired effect. Thrugg came to a halt at the middle of the bridge. The guard was taken aback by this and wondered what was going to happen next.

In his own, slow, deliberate way Thrugg considered the words of the challenge one by one. Finally he reached his conclusion and offered his reply to the guard: "I do not know the password, because I have never been told it. I'm not part of your band, you see. My companions and I have come here to rescue the King of Battenburgh you cruelly kidnapped. If you would like to hand him over, and surrender yourself to us, I'll see to it you get a fair trial before we hang you."

The guard was a quick thinker and it didn't take him anything like as long to formulate his reply. After all, the rest of Thrugg's friends had emerged from the shadows and were making their way towards the bridge. He delivered a quick "You don't know the trouble you're in!" before turning and rushing into the darkness of the tunnel that led away from the approaching forces of law and order. Obviously he was off to raise the alarm.

Eldon, about to lead the rest of them onto the bridge, watched him go in disbelief. "Thrugg," he shouted, "Surely you don't need me to tell you to get after, do you? But if you do, get after him!" Despite this clear instruction Thrugg remained rock like at the centre of the bridge. "Why aren't you going?" Eldon demanded with rising exasperation. "I don't seem to be able to move my feet," came the slow reply. As one, the party of friends looked at Thrugg's feet and realised that they couldn't see them any more.

His legs seemed to end in a tangle of purple and yellow roots that were engulfing his extra large feet. They appeared to come from beneath the bridge. Thrugg said when he saw them: "They weren't there when I stopped." Quickbeam gave a more scholarly considered opinion: "I believe those are the tentacles of the 'Big Hand'. You know, it's a creature that lives under bridges like these and waits for something tasty for lunch to come along. Last time I saw one of these was before Derfsgape. They're very rare you know."

Gerald's natural curiosity was aroused by this. Never being the one to think he knew everything he asked: "Why are they called 'Big Hands'?" Quickbeam went on to give the explanation: "It's because of its large hand like claws with which it gathers in its prey once it's trapped them." Gertrude couldn't believe her eyes. As Quickbeam gave his explanation the hand like claws appeared from under the edge of the bridge and began to try and pull Thrugg down to who knows what fate. "I think I could do with some help," came the plead as he was jerked off his feet and had to cling to the edge of the bridge to stop himself from being disappeared.

Again as one, his three friends dashed forward to add their strength to his own. Soon there were four bodies desperately avoiding a plunge into the depths that lay beneath the bridge. Only Quickbeam stood aloof. He seemed lost in thought at the edge of the chasm. As the tangle of bodies, hand like claws and tentacles moved ever closer to the edge "Will you come and help?" Gerald grunted. "That's what I'm trying to do." Quickbeam replied, "I'm trying to remember what worked last time." The tangle gave another jerk which made Gertrude bark: "You better remember NOW if you're going to make any difference!"

This instruction, heavily loaded as it was with hidden power, had the desired effect. Quickbeam's head went back as if it had been struck by a wet fish or some other inspiring and surprising object. His eyes glazed over. Those in the know knew that he was in that instant reliving the last encounter he had had with this fearsome creature. Automatically, unconsciously, his right hand grasped his spell book. Almost lifeless fingers rifled the pages. Unseeing eyes consulted the spell that was written there. Lips without their own volition gave unheard life to the spell. Out of nowhere came great globes of electric blue lightening which hurtled passed the struggling mass of people and creature and disappeared under the rock bridge. There was a soundless explosion that took everyone's breath away, followed by a moment of stillness that seemed to last for a month at least. Then, as suddenly as they had appeared, the tentacles disappeared back under the bridge leaving the heroes lying exhausted side by side.

Quickbeam came out of the trance that Gertrude had induced. "Got it" he said to no-one in particular. "The thick shell prevents any direct attack but it can be stunned with a 'Lightening Bolt'!" Turning to his spell book he was surprised to find that it was already open at the right page. Nevertheless he made ready to cast the spell. As he looked up to target it he realised the monster was no longer there. Then he realised that there was a blank spot in his memory. Feeling rather stupid he asked: "What did I do?"

Before Thrugg could even begin the blow by blow account that he would give in response to that question Gertrude injected with a quick: "Never mind that now. Let's get over this bridge before it wakes up." Swiftly the party made their way across the gap and were soon gathered where the guard had once stood.

As one they sank to the floor of the passageway to catch their breaths. Thrugg had finally completed another thought: "My ankles hurt," he said. Gertrude reached for her bag of healing bits and bobs as she looked at the offending parts. Sure enough blood was oozing through the trousers tucked into his boots. Daubing salve and ointments on the injuries Gertrude listened as her companions talked quietly together as they reviewed their progress in the dark so far.

Gerald was sharing some of his concerns. He believed that someone or something really powerful was behind all this. To have Acid Dogs as the first line of defence, backed up by a Big Hands next, spoke volumes to his experienced adventurer's instincts. Gerald counselled turning back and going for reinforcements. Eldon pooh-poohed this idea and boldly led them away from the bridge and started into what became a maze of tunnels and corridors beyond

He was brought to a shuddering halt as Thrugg hand grabbed him on the shoulder. The leader turned to look at his restraining friend. Thrugg was looking down the dark corridor that lay before. "Do you still want me to go after him Eldon?" he asked his leader. "Only I can't see him any more and I'm not sure I know the way to go." It took Eldon a few moments to realise that Thrugg was continuing the conversation that had preceded the encounter with the Big Hands. Thrugg was finally ready to go in pursuit of the guard who had fled into the darkness that now lay before them.

"Never mind him now," Eldon replied, once more firmly in control. "We'll all go together now they're expecting us. Battle formation team! Let's go!" Bravely he followed Thrugg leading the way to the expected fight. Quickbeam came next leaving Gerald and Gertrude standing side by side surveying the dark route ahead. They exchanged a glance which carried a thousand words, shrugged their shoulders at one another and started to follow their leader along the route he had chosen for them.

Very soon the party was faced with another decision. Once more there was a fork in the path. Eldon gave the instruction and Thrugg turned into the right hand tunnel. Another few yards and another junction had to be negotiated. And it wasn't long before there was yet another similar decision to be made.

Despite Eldon's confidence the other heroes followed him with a mixture of emotions and a variety of reactions. While their leader acted as if he knew where he was going, it was clear to the rest that they had entered a maze. And it was a complex maze designed to confuse and contain.

It was beginning to dawn on Gertrude and Gerald that there must be a purpose beyond simple delaying tactics to such a complex defence. There had to be something else. Before they could communicate these thoughts to Eldon, Thrugg walked around a bend in the corridor and came to a sudden dead stop. Eldon wasn't watching where he was going and walked into his back. Quickbeam added to the traffic jam as he was deep in spell book study. It was only Gerald and Gertrude who were alert enough to see what was happening.

All looked down the corridor at what had caused Thrugg to make his sudden stop. And all of them had the same reaction: surprise tinged with apprehension. They were staring into the hideous face of a gruesome creature dripping with slime and other foul juices. There were many tiny eyes on stalks scattered over the front of the monster before them. There was an expectant silence as everyone waited for someone else to say something. It fell to Thrugg to break the pregnant pause.

Clearly he had been thinking about whether or not he could recognise the creature. Once he had settled that question he would be able to deal with it. "No," he finally said, "I don't know what it is." There was another pause before he continued: "It might be friendly. What do you think?" Gerald chipped in with: "Is it dangerous?"

In answer to Thrugg's question Gertrude said that she thought she recognised it as a

Carrion Crawler. This worm like creature lived in tunnels and caverns such as these and really didn't have enough brains to be friendly - or hostile. It just simply got on with life as it saw it. In answer to Gerald's question she went on to say that she thought it ate anything that stumbled into its path. As that was they had just done they should consider it to be dangerous - particularly if it was hungry.

Quickbeam asked her if she knew how often it was hungry. She replied that the only time such a creature was not hungry was when it was eating. Then Quickbeam asked her what she thought they should do, she referred that upwards to Eldon, their noble leader. His considered reply was not long in coming.

And so our heroes were running down the maze of tunnels with the monster in hot pursuit of its lunch. One thing the party was good at doing was running away from danger when they had to. Gerald led the way - as any good scout should - and the others followed. At every turn there wasn't time for thought. They just plunged on down the widest and most traveled way.

After it seemed that they had been running for hours, although it was not more than a minute, Gerald became aware of something blocking the tunnel in front of him. As he drew closer he realised that it was moving only slightly slower than the fleeing party. He slowed the pace then slowed to match that of the blockage and took the time to take a closer look.

It took a while but Gerald finally recognized the yellow spotted green bulk of slime covered flesh that was before him. It was the tail end of the Carrion Crawler. The party had been running in a circle! But at least being that far in front of the biting end did give him a chance to have a look around while he ran.

In the side of the rock passageway Gerald spotted a narrow side passage. With a sharp side step he dived into that cleft. Gertrude squeezed in alongside him, closely followed by Quickbeam and the bulk of Thrugg. Gerald closed his eyes in frustration as Eldon continued to run away from and after the Carrion Crawler.

"He'll be back," Gerald said to no-one in particular and they all caught their breaths. Sure enough, in less than a minute the Carrion Crawler still pursing Eldon who was chasing the Carrion Crawler rushed passed the cleft's entrance. There was another pause before these events were once more repeated. Gertrude stepped in then for this was going too far. She uttered the single word "Gerald" so heavily loaded with meaning and menace that the scout was driven into action.

Despite that, Eldon went three more times around the loop before Gerald was finally able to catch hold of him and drag him to the safety of their hiding place.

Unfortunately by then their leader had begun to tire and the Carrion Crawler was close enough to get hold of an arm and try to pull Eldon back. Luckily it was at this point that Thrugg intervened. With a single blow to the monster's nose his leader was free. The Carrion Crawler recoiled in shock before angrily striking at the party once more.

This is when Gerald stepped into the fray. He placed his sword by the neck of the beast which halted the lunge. A short conversation then ensued. Gerald explained how flesh, even Carrion Crawler's flesh, could be terminally damaged by the application of cold steel. He went on to apologise that he and his comrades had disturbed the creature. He explained that they meant it no harm and, apart from the single fist blow from Thrugg, they had caused no lasting damage. However, the scout went on, trapped in this crack as they now were, if it came to a fight an awful lot of damage would be done before the conflict was resolved. Gerald encouraged the creature to consider this before making any further threatening move.

Gertrude was transfixed by this confrontation. She had no idea if the beast even understood a word that Gerald was saying. She didn't even know if Gerald knew. But her friend just kept on talking in a measured and calm way, attempting to defuse the situation. She began to wonder if Zama had been giving him lessons. She was going to have to watch out!

Whether or not the monster understood what Gerald had been saying to it, the sentiment of the message must have penetrated to creatures brain. Either that or it had realised the impossibility of arguing with the sword at its face. With great difficulty it sucked itself back into the main tunnel and squelched off away from the cleft. It had clearly decided to go elsewhere in the tunnels and feast on rodent rather than human flesh.

There was a collective sigh of relief and once more the band sank to the floor to recover their breaths. Once more Gertrude's bag of healing was called into service to patch up more minor injuries that had passed unnoticed in the headlong flight. Quickbeam had the gaping wound on his shoulder expertly stitched using twisted cobwebs. Thrugg had the gash on his left calf cleaned and packed with moss. Eldon had the broken finger nail filed. Then Gertrude looked for her friend, the scout, confident that there was nothing wrong with him. It was then that the band realised that Gerald was nowhere to be seen.

He had moved deeper into the cleft while all these necessary running repairs were going on. He was intent on doing what any good scout should always do - looking around for danger or any other opportunity. He had reasoned that if this cleft was not a dead end, it must lead somewhere. It was best to know where that was - and what was there - as soon as possible. Gerald wasn't confident about having to outwit the carrion Crawler again but there were worst things than carrion Crawlers. It was just as Gertrude was looking for him to see if he needed any patching up that he once more emerged out of the shadows to address his friends.

"We're in luck," he reported, "There's a lot of doors down here. It looks like we've found the hideout." That got everyone's attention. Hideout means bandits and bandits mean treasure - not to mention a king to be rescued. It didn't take long for them to get organised. Battle ready with all the caution of the highly skilled adventurers they were, they were sooner moving down the cleft to see what Gerald had found. Although they started forward in almost total darkness it was not long before they could see that the far end of the cleft was lit by a yellowish light. It was then only a matter of moments before they emerged from the narrow split in the rock wall and took up cautious positions in the rock tunnel that it opened out into.

The party looked up and down the tunnel. At regular intervals there were candle lanterns mounted on the side walls. In most of these a candle burned. These were the source of the yellowish light. By each of the lanterns there was a door. As far as they could see there was nothing to distinguish one door from the next. In one direction the doors and their accompanying lanterns ran out after only two. The tunnel ran on beyond the last pool of candlelight into darkness. It was at this junction of light and dark that Gerald had taken post. He was concentrating while the rest, quietly and wrapped in stillness, left him to his appointed task.

Slowly Gerald turned to address his companions: "I think it leads to the outside," he reported. "As far as I can see and hear - and smell - there's nothing else down there. If there are any guards to creatures they're being very still and very quiet - and they've had a bath recently." Most of his companions smiled at this but Thrugg, in his imponderable way, mulled over this report. In the end he gave voice to the question that formed in his mind: "Are you sure you can't smell the soap they used?" he asked his sneaky companion.

Gertrude laid a gentle hand on one of his tree trunk arms. "Not now," she said. Thrugg acknowledged the gentle instruction with a slight nod of his head and resumed his cautious watch down the lighted half of the tunnel. Now everyone waited for their leader to make the decision. It took a while but finally Eldon got the message: "We'll start at this end and work that way," he instructed. Gerald gave a nod and turned to inspect the large iron lock set into the banding on the last – or first, depending on your point of view - door.

In a jiffy the lock was picked and, upon receiving the nod from their leader, the adventurers piled into the room. The door had opened onto a small cave no more than 20 feet long. The sides had been fitted with rough wooden shelves. These were piled high with a variety of sacks and baskets. Small barrels were stacked on all the available floor space. It didn't take long to establish that this was the cave system dweller's food store. "No treasure here - although Rogo might be interested in the ale," Gerald thought to himself. At a sign from Eldon the party moved on to the next door.

This was not locked. As soon as it was thrown open the party piled in. They all felt rather foolish. It was, after all, a small, dark, rather smelly, latrine. Sheepishly the adventurers extracted themselves and moved on to the next door. Weapon store, empty bunk room and deserted common room were discovered and discarded. When the next door was opened our heroes could not believe their eyes.

This was no cave with rocky walls. This was no store room or chamber moulded to a communal purpose. This chamber was palatial after the crudeness of what had gone before. The walls were hung with deep red rich velvet. The floor was covered with furs which were so deep that any dwarves or hobbits might have had problems finding their way across it. The room was lit by oil lamps of the finest quality and the rest of the furnishings spoke of opulence.

The room was dominated by a large bed. It was covered with many cushions of different shapes and colours. Nestling amid these was a young lady. Her beauty was such that the male members of the party were stopped in their tracks. Everyone knew that this was going to be no normal encounter. Thrugg looked confused as he tried to work out what had happened. How had he stumbled into this lady's bedchamber? Gerald was clearly engaged in a complex series of calculations but it would have taken another skilled scout to work out whether it was with the furnishings in the room or its occupant that was the focus of his considerations. There was no mistaking Gertrude's view. She looked on with contempt. How could a woman demean herself so much? Nevertheless a close look at the healer's eyes showed that she was wary and ready for anything as she scanned the room.

Quickbeam and Eldon seemed ready for anything as well. But their object of attention was the young lady reclining on the bed. Her beauty had captivated the magic users mind and Eldon was simply entranced by what was below him.

The adventurers simply stood there and waited for someone else to make the first move. And as they waited the electricity and tension in the room grew and grew. Someone was going to have to make the first move. One thing was certain. It wasn't going to be the young lady. Her eyes were moving from party member to party member and the tightness in the air grew and grew.

And then Eldon spoke ...

Chapter 7: Capture

Well, Eldon tried to speak. He opened his mouth to utter some amazingly seductive words but all that emerged was a variation on his familiar stutter. "Huh ... huh ... huh," he said. He was simply entranced by the young lady sitting on her bed, alluring and attractive. Lost completely in the beauty before him, Eldon was unable to find the words.

Gertrude was quick to show her contempt for the situation. With a toss of her head she turned to her friend the scout and whispered an aside: "I suppose its better than the usual 'goat' impression!" It took every ounce of his self-control to prevent Gerald from laughing out loud. Gertrude dug him in the ribs with her elbow and the hissed instruction to "do something".

And so it was that Gerald stepped in to fill the void. First he placed a gentle restraining hand onto his leader's shoulder. Startled by the physical intrusion Eldon's eyes cleared a little and he looked round. Seeing his companion looking at him Eldon began to realize where he was and what had happened over the last few minutes. He tried to explain, indicating the young lady who was still waiting patiently and alluring on the other side of the room. Still all that would come out was "Huh ... Huh ... Huh." Gerald raised a restraining palm and spoke gently to his leader. "Perhaps you'd better leave this to me," he suggested. Still unable to speak Eldon simply nodded his consent.

Gerald turned to the young lady and gave her one of his 'special' smiles. The beauty rewarded this by focusing all of her not inconsiderable attentions onto the scout. Encouraged Gerald, extruding charm from every pore, began to cross the room towards the object of desire still lying amongst the cushions as they had discovered her.

He got to within about six feet before he stopped. Taking an easy stance, he addressed her with his usual boyish charm. "Hallo my pretty little lady. My name's Gerald and I'm sure we're going to get on famously," was his opening gambit. This was rewarded with a smile and the beauty shifted her position, making herself more comfortable and alluring at the same time.

Gerald felt a sweat breaking out on his forehead. Even with all his experience he was finding it hard to resist the obvious charms. A quick glance over his shoulder confirmed that his companions were now completely entranced. Eldon had gone all glazed eyed again. Thrugg stood motionless with his mouth slightly open. Quickbeam had been rummaging amongst his pockets and pouches. Now he held a shiny red apple and seemed to be about to offer as a gift. Only Gertrude remained detached. Her contempt was clear to see. When her eyes met Gerald's the instructions were clear: Get on with it! And that's what he did.

He turned once more to face the young lady. He was about to continue the conversation when she beat him to the draw. Her voice was deep and husky as she gave him his instructions. "Come closer," she said. There was such raw power in those two words that Gerald even took half a pace forward before he checked himself. Now it was his turn to wonder if Zama had been giving lessons. He settled himself once more. Regaining his composure, he responded with "But what about them?"

The young lady turned her head to one side as she considered the question. Gerald felt the sweat burst out with a greater force. He knew he was potentially in deep trouble - and very nice trouble it was too. Finally after an age the reply came. "Them too," she said. Thrugg immediately started forward only stopping when Gertrude laid a hand on his shoulder. Hearing the movement Gerald glanced briefly behind him and noted that his healing companion had switched onto high alert. That immediately produced a similar reaction in him. They had been companions too long to ignore one another's adventuring instincts. If Gertrude sensed danger it was time to be ready for anything. Unfortunately Eldon and Quickbeam missed these signals completely.

Eldon was striding across the room wiping his hands on his trousers as preparation to greeting the lady as the gentleman he liked to think he was. Quickbeam was eagerly offering his apple as he moved closer like a schoolboy determined to please his favorite teacher. Only Gerald remained motionless as caution replaced attraction in the midst of the highly charged atmosphere. In no time at all Gerald had been past by two of his three male companions. They stood side by side at the foot of the bed like puppies eager to please their mistress who was lying before them.

Gerald was about to make a suggestion for a quick exit to Gertrude when the beauty laughed out loud. The tone of that sound was such that for a moment everyone was frozen. Into that pause that she had created the young lady spoke a single word: "Now." Suddenly the stillness was replaced by organised chaos.

The first thing that happened was that the rich, red drapes that seemed to be covering the wall behind the bed on which the young lady lay were wrenched from their rails. Suddenly the chamber was twice as large as it had been. The extra space was filled with men. They were armed to the teeth and ready for action. In the shadows at the back stood the one who was obviously their leader. Although he could only be dimly seen it was clear that he was wearing clothes of quality. Black leather covered most of his flesh from the finely tooled boots to the jerkin with just the right amount of trimmings. His face was hidden by the shadows in which he lurked but his voice spoke with authority as he ordered his minions forward.

Then the rest of the room was filled with action. Thrugg, for all his apparent slowness and bulk, knew what he had to do in situations like this. He moved in front of Gertrude and drew his huge two handed sword. The speed with which he wielded it in the confines of the room it made it almost impossible for anyone to get close to him or the healer he was protecting. At least three of the bandits fell clutching serious wounds as they attempted to approach the swordsman.

Quickbeam reacted almost as quickly. The apple, which was to be his offering to the fair maiden, was hurled across the room almost before the drapes had hit the floor. One of the bandits was felled by the missile. Next he was delving desperately into the pockets and pouches of his robes while summoning phrases of power to his lips. With confidence he spoke the words of incantation and threw some material components at two more of the approaching bandits. The result stopped them in their tracks - but not for long. They were surprised to be engulfed in a cloud of bubbles but totally unaffected by them.

Quickbeam was desperately rethinking his situation. He had hoped to contain them in a bubble of null time but under the pressure seemed to have recalled a spell he had created for amusing the village children instead. Having no time to come up with another magical defence to the onslaught, Quickbeam drew his dagger. He knew that the bandits would have the advantage of reach with their swords but he wasn't going to make it easy for them.

Eldon was perhaps the slowest to react, entranced as he was by the beauty of the young woman who had lured them into this trap. However, as soon as he saw that his mage was in trouble instinct took over. He leaped across the room to place himself between Quickbeam and the advancing bandits. Once more they paused in their strides now that they were faced by the chain mail clad leader of this band. He was a much more difficult prospect than a befuddled mage.

Gerald, as might be expected of his craft, was the quickest to react. Almost before the 'Now' was out of the temptress's lips he simply wasn't there any more. It's not exactly clear how he does it but as befits any senior member of the Scouts Guild he had learnt to disappear at will in almost any situation or circumstances. He used this ability to great personal benefit. He hadn't bought a round of drinks in years. And while he always maintained that it was simply keeping his skills at their maximum potential, that excuse was beginning to wear thin with his companions.

But he was making good use of his skills now as he passed invisibly amongst the battle for survival that was unfolding. His instincts had told him from the moment that the curtains had gone down that this was a lost cause. No matter how hard they fought, he and his friends were going to lose. His best plan was to make sure that he could escape so that afterwards he could seek revenge on those who were attacking them. In some cold, dark, recess of his mind he knew that each one of them would die, slowly and painfully, as payment for the death of his friends.

He was halfway to the door when the bandit leader said something that gave him hope. "Take them all alive," came the instruction and Gerald smiled a cold smile to himself as he moved on his not seen journey. Now he knew it was imperative that he got away so that he could return and rescue his friends. He slipped out of the door and started running down the corridor in the direction that he had determined led to the outside world. This meant that he missed the conclusion of the confrontation.

First to fall was Eldon. He was swiftly disarmed by one of the bandits in front of him. Then two more simply log piled him to the floor where the consciousness was beaten from him. Eldon conqueror had turned his attention to Quickbeam. By simply pointing the point of his sword at the wizard's throat he had backed him up against one of the walls of the room. Quickbeam dropped the dagger that had proved as useless as he knew it was going to be. "Maybe we can talk about this ..." he began. The bandit in front of him silenced him by simply punching on the chin. Quickbeam crumbled to the floor like a fallen tree.

Thrugg was proving a more difficult proposition. His sword had already felled a further two of the bandits before they got organised. Three of them had picked up a bench and used that as a shield and battering ram. Using this they were able to force Thrugg back and hamper his sword arm. Gertrude was pinned behind him. There was nothing either of them could do as another of the bandits simply pounded Thrugg to the floor with a stool.

Gertrude had not choice. She surrendered with all the grace she could muster. The bandits stripped her of anything that might have been useful and tightly bound her hands behind her back. She watched, always vigilant for any opportunity. She saw the bandit leader step forward from the shadows. He stood alongside the young lady who had led them into the trap. The healer watched with revulsion as the two villains looked at one another with attraction in their eyes.

The revulsion grew as they smiled at one another with a warmth not shared by the onlooker. It reached its greatest depths as the leader peeled off one of his gloves to stroke the face of the young lady. Despite the obvious warmth between Gertrude could only feel cold in the pit of her stomach. The left hand was grotesque although the young lady writhed in pleasure under its touch. Then, suddenly, a memory stirred deep in the healer's mind. And it was not a pleasant one. She'd seen that hand before. She couldn't quite remember the circumstances but knew she had to remember.

The struggle to recall a long forgotten thought was broken as Thrugg was hauled to his feet by four of the bandits. He too had been tightly bound but his continuing struggles meant that Gertrude and her captors had to make great efforts to keep their balance. Once a resemblance of order has been restored there were other pressing matters for the adventurers. The bandit leader had left his female co-conspirator and moved across the room to inspect his captives. Gertrude could feel her revulsion again as it looked like he was going to stroke her cheek with the same grotesque hand.

Before that happened something had caught the leader's attention. He looked from the captives to the captors. "What's missing?" he asked. The question received blank stares from the men who only moments before had been enjoy the warmth of the fellowship that their triumph had brought. They looked from one to another, seeking a volunteer to give voice to their collective opinion. In the end one of them found voice enough to mutter: "Sorry boss. We don't know."

"When they came into the room there were five of them. You've managed to capture four," the leader explained. "Somehow one of them managed to slip out of this careful prepared trap. It's got to be their scout - and quite a skilful one at that." The other bandits looked from one to another as they felt their confidence slipping away. Overcoming fighters and mages was one thing. Trapping a highly skilled scout was an entirely different prospect. They were not looking forward to it.

"You four bring those four along," the leader continued, "and the rest of you get out there after him." The majority of the bandits wished they had been chosen for the escort duty. They were inspecting their boots to see if they were fit for the job, reluctant to embark on their instructed task. "GO!" bellowed the leader, "and don't come back without him! We'll join you as soon as I seen this lot secured."

He watched with satisfaction as his men scuttled out on their mission. With a head gesture he indicated that those that were left should follow him and bring their charges with them. Eldon, Thrugg, Quickbeam and Gertrude were bundled along one of the rock lined tunnels as the leader strode in front as master of the domain. Each one of the adventurers wondered what fate awaited them. The answer was not long coming.

Chapter 8: Thwarted Escape
Continued

Eldon swung by his wrists that were tied to the beam high in the laboratory where he had been led. He had listened carefully to the account of the adventure so far given to him by his companions. Now he reflected on what he had heard and came to a conclusion. To no one in particular he said: "So, that's how we ended up here."

His companions simply hung there, twisting slowly from side by their restrained wrists, each one of them lost in their own thoughts. In the end it was Gertrude who broke the silence. "Just as long as I know," she said. There was another pause before she continued: "You know, I don't think I'm going to put us back together after this one." The silence deepened and the room felt a little colder as her companions digested this information.

Remarkably it was Thrugg who broke the silence. "She was a very pretty young lady," he said. His companions were confused. It seemed that Thrugg had already given up and written off Gertrude, consigning her to an unknown but terminal fate. Eldon was clearly confused. Well, let's be honest, it didn't take much to confuse Eldon! In the end he gave voice to his confusion. "Thrugg," he said, "Just who are you going on about?"

"That girl in the room with the red curtains," the warrior replied. "I liked her." Quickbeam was indignant. "How can you say that?" he demanded. "She used all her feminine charms to lure us into a trap. And when it was sprung she just lay there and watched as we were taken. And then she laughed in obvious pleasure at our misfortune when that man joined her to gloat over his victory. How can you possibly admire her?"

There was a pause as this tirade worked its way through the labyrinth of Thrugg's thought processes. In the end he conclusion was reached. "Everything you say Quickbeam is true," he concluded. "But leaving all that to one side, think back and remember what you saw when you were going to give her that apple. She was a very pretty young lady." This provoked another long pause amongst the captives as they put themselves back in the room with the red curtains.

Finally, it was Eldon who once more broke the silence. "Yes Thrugg," he agreed, "She was very pretty. That's why the trap worked." Gertrude chipped in with "And you men were so stupid to be fooled by a pretty face!" Both of these added to Quickbeam's fury. So he turned his anger on their scout. "And you're not much help either," he said. "I thought you'd managed to get away and go for help!"

Gertrude decided that it was time to chide her friend for his failure as well, pitching in with: "Yes, but here you are like the perennial bad penny." She waited for her friend's repost which she knew would lighten the darkness of the group's current mood. After a while she realised that nothing was coming. "What's the matter?" she asked. "You've been very quiet. Cat got your tongue or something?"

Her trusty friend replied. "Not yet," he said, " and he's not having it either. Not if I have my way." Once more Eldon was confused. It was he who broke the fresh silence. "What are you going on about?" he asked. His trusty scout explained as if he was addressing a small child: "I mean I've just managed to free my wrists and all I need now is to get my hand on one of my daggers and in a minute we'll all be out of here."

The mood amongst the adventurers lightened somewhat with those words. For the first time since they had been lured into the trap there was a collective feeling of hope. The gloom in the laboratory that was their holding cell before who knew what had lightened somewhat.

It was then that the door of the cavern crashed opened.

Chapter 9: Escape Renewed.

The door slammed against the rock wall. It had clearly been pushed with some force to add drama to the re-emergence of the bandits. The band of thugs strode purposefully into the room carrying lit lanterns and the room grew brighter as they took their positions. One by one they entered the room and lined the walls on each side of the door. They leered at their captives hanging helplessly before them. Eager anticipation was in their eyes. One or two of them were clearly seen to be licking their lips. Whether it was bravado on their part, or designed to add even more dejection to the adventurers, or a genuine expression of their victory, was not clear. They stood, silent, threatening, leering, waiting for something to happen. It was not long before it did.

Out of the comparative darkness of the corridor beyond came a figure. He was dressed in his trademark black with just the hint of white and red piping to mark him out from a common villain. The situation confirmed this. No common crook could have worked such as trap as this to ensnare some of Sham's finest heroes. Everyone knew this and acknowledged the situation in their own way.

The adventurers felt any hope that had been born in them only a few moments before drain away. Each one's shoulders sagged lower and they hung more heavily from the beam to which they had been tied. If they choose to look at the bandit band and their leader who had captured them it was with hooded eyes that spoke of the defeat they all felt.

The bandits now stood tall and proud. They knew they were the finest specimens of outlaw talent that could be found in any part of the underworld of this region. Now they were going to savour the fruits of their victory. These, their most powerful enemies before them, were going to be eliminated and then the region was going to be theirs for the taking. Good times were on their way.

The leader simply stood quietly assessing the situation. He was using the moment to impress his personality upon his captives. First he looked around his men. This was a look of approval acknowledged by a straightening of backs and raising of heads. He saw that his men were ready and eager to do his bidding. Then he turned his attention to the captives.

One by one he looked at them. With each he was careful to look into the eyes of his captured prey so that they knew all hope was gone. Their defeat was total. He examined his victims with contempt.

First Eldon came under his inspection. Without his chain mail and the usual array of adventuring kit he was just another man hanging from his wrists. The finest linen shirt he wore was stained and torn as a result of the rough treatment that had been handed out on his way to this place. The hair was in a terrible state that would have caused him some great distress. However, under the gaze of his captor Eldon knew that he had bigger things than his hair to worry about. He was going to have to come up with some plan if he had any chance of keeping his head.

The bandit leader discounted his counterpart and let his eyes move on to the next prisoner. This was Thrugg. Here, at least, was someone seemingly unmoved by the predicament he found himself in. Despite the blood still oozing from the various cuts inflicted during his capture and the obvious discomfort of his physical restraint, this warrior seemed detached from the circumstances. At first the bandit leader thought that danger lurked behind this person's eye. It was if he was meditating on some plan to turn the tables, or at least some ploy designed to lead to the escape of himself and his colleagues. After a time the bandit realised that this was not the case. This warrior only had one purpose - to carry out orders in as complete and forceful manner that he could. Finally a decision was taken in the mind of the bandit chief. Maybe this one could be turned and prove a valuable member of the gang. Thoughts were set in motion seeking a lever in which to bring about that turning.

Meanwhile the eyes had moved on to the lady of the bunch. She was clearly that and nothing that had happened to her in the last hour or so had diminished her obvious status. The leader had to acknowledge that. In a way he admired it as well.

It was when their eyes met that recognition finally flooded into Gertrude's memory. It took every ounce of her natural ability and her intensive training honed by the fires of experience to keep that fact from her captor. Despite the immaculate disguise that was his hallmark, Gertrude, like Gerald before her, had come to realise that she was at the mercy of Luther d'Eth, bandit extraordinaire and scourge of Sham. She knew that the only hope for them all was to appear not to know who he was so that she could use her knowledge against him.

She thought back to the very first time she had met him. That, too, was in the depths of a cave system. She and her fellows were searching for the mage Mandrake who had gone missing. It happened regularly after a good night in "The Portly Pixie" and a few flagons of honeymead. Mandrake was always desperate to sleep in his own bed and insisted that a short cut through the woods would be quicker than finding his way down the Capital road.

Of course, the woods were always full of orcs. The ones who lived closest to Sham had been domesticated somewhat thanks to the constant attentions of Rogo, Zama and the rest of the Militia. However, it was accepted that once the sun had gone down, the woods were their domain. Anyone who happened to pass that way was fair game. Lost traveller, foolish hunter or drunken mage were all the same to the tribes who made their homes amid the trees. The taking of hostages was those orcs main source of income.

The time Gertrude was recalling as she hung in the laboratory started out just like any other mission to rescue Mandrake. Zama had added the usual amount to his tab and sent a small rescue force to deliver coin and return the mage. However, after a morning visiting the tribal homelands, Mandrake was not to be found in the possession of any of the usual suspects. The rescue party had had to fall back on their adventuring skills. Gerald who was scouting for them even then followed Mandrake's tracks to where he was overcome by a band of orcs and onward into a cave system occupied by nobody as far as they knew.

Going forward into the darkness had led them to the very orcs who probably captured Mandrake. After dispatching them - for they had no interest in any conversation - the adventuring band had pressed on in their search for the careless mage. And find him they did - trapped within a magical field of force that took all their collective ingenuity to overcome. Instead of escaping at this point the wizard dragged them further into the depths of the cave system.

This was when Gertrude met Luther for the first time. In a room lined with what appeared to be stone statues they confronted this villain. It seemed that he was intent on destroying what little law and order existed in the region of Sham and wanted to recruit Mandrake to assist him with that. Gertrude, Mandrake and the rest were having none of this. They decided it was time to bring this kidnapper to justice - dead or alive.

That was when the true nature of the statue became apparent. They were in fact stone golems manufactured by Springfever. As the adventurers closed in Luther had uttered the words of power. The golems started moving and attacking all within the room. Chaos was everywhere as the fight for survival ensued. And in that chaos Luther escaped unnoticed. Still Gertrude and her friends had found Mandrake - not to mention a readily portable amount of treasure.

From that day forward he had been a thorn in the side of everyone who worked for the good of the community of Sham. He had been behind several mysterious events in and around the village, but as a master of disguise so his deformed guiding hand had sometimes only been seen by those who had the eyes to see. Oh yes, Gertrude remembered Luther.

From the look of lust in his eyes it was clear that Luther remembered Gertrude as well. So close so many times before and now he had her in his grasp. But it was clear that Luther was going to savor his moment of victory. Gertrude watched as with some difficulty he let his eyes drift further along the line. She was forgotten for a moment while he inspected Quickbeam.

Clearly Luther was looking at a mage - and a highly skilled one at that. But as with all such practitioners there was a distraction that could be used to dull their wits and distract their minds. With Mandrake it was honeymead, with Quickbeam it was a pretty face. Luther gazed at his captive. It was clear that he would need some conditioning to enhance his usefulness. Pain was a good stimulus in this area. Luther was clearly thinking this was where he was going to make his start.

It was around about now that Gertrude remembered something else. She heard again in her head what Gerald had been saying as the door to the chamber had burst open. Something had to be done to stop Luther's eyes continuing their journey along the line of prisoners. She decided that there was no other way for it. She needed to be the focus of Luther's attention for the next few minutes. Even with her hands tie to a beam above her head, she still had the subtle skills of her craft. It was time to use them again.

Although the movement was ever so slight and the sound that she made ever so quiet, they had the desired effect. The attention of not only Luther but of all the bandits lining the walls was drawn towards the seemingly helpless female before them. At last Luther came closer to his prisoners. He moved to stand directly in front of Gertrude. The look on his face changed from the pleasure of victory into one that spoke of the anticipation of excitement. He half raised his hand before he got himself back under control.

He turned his back on Gertrude and retreated a couple of paces. Once more he turned to face her. Now the look in his eyes showed that his mind had been made up. Something was going to happen. It was going to involve Gertrude and Luther. One of them was going to find it very pleasant, the other one was going to be revolted by it.

Luther turned to his henchmen. He lifted with gloved right hand and pointed it straight at Gertrude. "That one first," he instructed. The men smirked and moved forward. Soon the healer had been untied and thrust into the waiting arms of their leader. He took her towards the workbench that was alongside the door to the chamber.

"No! No! Take your filthy hands of me!" she cried as she was being dragged across the laboratory. This came as a surprise to Eldon still hanging by his wrists. It just didn't sound like Gertrude. He looked at his companions Thrugg, Quickbeam and then realised what Gertrude had remembered. It was clear the others had seen it too. Suddenly in the depths of their darkest hour of defeat there was a glimmer of hope.

Luther was pinning Gertrude to the workbench. He was filled with suppressed anticipation mixed with open lust. He was going to enjoy the next few minutes. Gertrude was looking up into his eyes. Her expression was everything you would expect from a helpless female. No matter how out of character it was for her at least it was holding Luther's attention. The other bandits were also engrossed in the drama being played out before them.

Then Gertrude's face changed. Luther put it down to submission. She had finally resigned herself to the events that were about to unfold. He removed his left glove and reached out with his deformed left hand to stroke the cheek of the object of his immediate desire. Gertrude stopped his hand by saying "You'll be sorry for this." There was something about the tone of her voice that just didn't ring true in the circumstances. He became even more worried someone spoke, interrupting his anticipation of enjoyment to come.

"Excuse me," came the voice from the far end of the chamber. It sounded like Gerald's. Luther turned like the panther he was to look at where the voice was coming from. His henchmen turned in the same direction but with a slowness that revealed the differences in the speeds of their minds. They all saw that it was Gerald.

Having freed himself of his bonds and covered by the distraction that Gertrude had provided, he had made his way to the large workbench that was situated at that far end of the laboratory. He was now standing in front of that bench. In each hand he held a large glass flask that he had selected at random from the mass of similar vessels ranged on the bench behind him. One was full of red liquid, the other blue. He looked back at the bandits and their leader with a quizzical expression. Now he had their attention. Every eye was watching his every move. The scout continued "I was wondering what would happen if I was to mix these two liquids together?"

The initial reaction amongst the bandits reflected their state of knowledge about the contents of the flasks. The henchmen were confused looking back and forth from the scout to their leader in the hope of getting some clear direction. Luther's face, however, was showing genuine fear. Gerald knew that he had chosen well from amongst the flasks. A smile came to his face reflecting his growing confidence that the tables had been turned.

Luther's reaction to that smile was instant. He knew that he had lost this encounter. His fear grew deeper as he stuttered "Please ... don't do that ... because ..." Gerald's look that moved from Luther to Gertrude who now standing in front of their captor with her back to him. He watched intently as she mouthed something to him. "Do it!" she said. Gerald was quick to oblige. His smile grew even wider as, with a "Ooops!" he released the two flasks.

Everyone was watching intently as they fell towards the floor. It was if they were falling in slow motion. Only when they struck the slabs that made up the base of this cavern did things speed up again. The flasks both smashed with a resounding crash and tinkle. The two liquids mixed together and suddenly the room was filling with acrid, choking smoke.

This induced panic amongst the bandits. They didn't know what to do next and all started running around like headless chickens. Some were trying to open the door to flee, forgetting that it opened inwards. The resulting pile up prevented any further progress in that direction. Others were desperately searching for something to put over their noses and mouths to prevent the fumes overcoming them. A few moved closer to Luther to seek his guidance. All they got there was the opportunity to see his reaction to the recent events. He was now displaying total and utter dejection. They heard him say ".. because they will explode," completing an early statement that had been overtaken by events. It was clear even their leader was having difficulty in deciding what was going to be the next best course of action.

Gertrude was certainly not going give her captors any chance to regroup or seize the initiative again. Suddenly she struck and one of the guards was falling to the floor with a mortal wound in his stomach. His face showed the surprise that Luther and the other shared as to where she had managed to conceal the dagger. Too late Luther realised it was his. She must have stolen it from his belt earlier.

Having seen his mate fall before him another of the henchmen made a flying leap at the woman. It was if she was expecting it. Gertrude ducked as he came towards her in the air. Then, grabbing him by the tunic, she gave him a helping hand so that his head struck the wall of the cavern with a fearsome blow. He crumbled to the floor in a heap and was clearly going to be out of action for some time.

Amid the growing confusion Luther stood aghast. Even his finely honed mind seemed to have closed down for a second. Gertrude used this momentary pause to relieve him of his sword pulling it from its scabbard. This added to his confusion as he felt it go. But, before he could do anything about it, he had another problem. With a skill born out her knowledge of human anatomy Gertrude struck at Luther's head. This single blow hit him with precision. His head spun and all that he could see were stars as the darkness grew about him. He crumbled to the floor as that darkness grew.

Having eliminated the leader for a time Gertrude got on with organising her comrades in the neutralization of the rest of the bandits. She tossed the dagger the length of the room to Gerald. He wasn't expecting it but managed instinctively to catch it. Gertrude saw that his look was asking what he should do with it. Despite being occupied with keeping two of the bandits away from herself with Luther's sword Gertrude still had time to shout to her friend the instruction "Free the others!"

Understanding dawned in the scouts mind. "Gotaya!" he shouted before turning to his friends still tied to the beam. However, any further progress in that direction was blocked by two of the brighter bandits. They were coming towards him with drawn swords. Gerald's immediate reaction that this was going to be no problem. He was armed now and he could take them. Then doubt began to creep into his mind as he compared the length of his dagger with that of both of the swords. Once more he looked at the other end of the room to get guidance from his friend.

There he saw that Gertrude was in some trouble. The leaping guard from earlier had recovered and was now trying to wrestle her to the ground. It was only the sword that she was holding that was preventing this from happening. Gerald also saw that things were about to get much worse. Luther had regained his feet and was about to grab her from behind. Training took over in Gerald's mind. Protect the healer! Save his friend! It took him a moment to make ready. Once he had shaped for the throw, the dagger was immediately flying across the chamber. It embedded itself into Luther's right arm. Once more Luther was heading floorwards. This time he was clutching his arm in pain.

"Gottcha!" Gerald thought to himself, "Now, about the rest of us." Once more he turned towards his friends. The sword wielding bandits were closer now and it was clear their confidence was growing. However, Gerald could see something behind them that made the smile return to his lips. Thinking it was the old 'look behind you' trick the stalking bandits rejected this option with small shakes of their heads. Gerald returned the gesture and added "You'll be sorry."

While the bandits were digesting this there came from behind them an almighty roar. What Gerald had seen was that Thrugg had decided it was time to show that there hadn't been the rope made that could withstand his formidable strength. Harder and harder he had strained. Suddenly the bonds had broken and he had greeted his freedom with the roar.

As the bandits turned to see what had made the noise they felt their feet leave the floor. Thrugg was simply picking one up in each hand. They just about had time to work this out before darkness closed about them. Thrugg simply banged their heads together until they stopped moving.

At the far end of the room Luther was slowly coming to his feet once more. He surveyed the scene before him. Gertrude was in the process of finishing off the leaping guard who had proved so troublesome. Thrugg had dropped his first victims and was stalking another two of the henchmen who were still conscious. Gerald had finally got himself organised and was laying about him with something heavy that he had picked up off the workbench behind him. It didn't take a mind as fine as Luther's to see that all was lost. With a shrug of his shoulders that seemed to say 'Ah, what's the use!' Luther conceded defeat. He slinked across the room and out of the door leaving his band to their inevitable fate.

The end was not long coming. Gerald and Thrugg soon polished off the rest of the leaderless and demoralised bandits. This left Gertrude to free Eldon and Quickbeam. Then searched for her first aid kit and set to work putting Thrugg back together again.

Unnoticed by the others, Gerald was searching the room. Under some sacking beneath one of the workbenches he had discovered a large iron bound chest. Once he had dragged it into the open it was the work of moments for him to pick the lock. He carefully lifted the lid, wary of the possibility of traps, and his eyes grew wide as he stared at the contents.

"Hey! Look what I've found!" he called to his friends. Knowing their scout well his friends were soon clustered around the chest. It was full of treasure. Gemstones, coins, silver trinkets and other valuable items were almost spilling from the edges. It fell to Eldon to voice to their collective thoughts. "There must be a King's ransom here," he said. There was a collective nodding of heads as hands started transferring the best items to sacks and pouches for homeward transportation. Then a thought struck Quickbeam.

"Speaking of the King, we never did find him did we?" he said. Gerald and Gertrude exchanged a look that only they understood. They had worked out what had been going on and knew there was no king to find. It was clear they were going to keep that a secret from the others for now. However, Quickbeam had continued with his reflection as he looked around the chamber. He continued by asking "And where did the leader go?"

Thrugg was able to provide the answer to that one. Once more he showed that he was not as stupid as he appeared. "He slipped out the door in the middle of the fight," he explained to anyone who was really interested. Eldon, still busy stuffing things into a sack, resumed his role of leader by stating "It doesn't matter. Where ever he is we've seen the last of him. Let's get this lot back to the Inn."

The rest of the adventurers agreed as they continued gathering up their treasure. It didn't take long for the task to be completed and the heroes were very soon leaving the laboratory for their return journey to Sham.

Chapter 10: A Triumphant Return

Evening was drawing on and Stumpy was moving around the common room of the Portly Pixie lighting the lamps. He was using the 'Create Fire' that Mandrake had taught him. All was going well until he came to the table where Malifest, Markenbrat and the dwarves from the castle building gang were sleeping off their lunch - from yesterday. Stumpy was obviously nervous in the presence of such an experienced and proficient wizard as the elf prince. So much so that his concentration must have wandered a little. The first the orc knew about it was when the beard belonging to one of the dwarven masons sitting next to Markenbrat burst into flames instead of the wick in the lamp.

Still consumed with panic Stumpy looked for something to put out the flaming facial hair. He grabbed the pitcher of stale beer from the centre of the table and poured it over the dwarf's head. The fire went out and the dwarf slept on. Stumpy breathed a sigh of relief and continued on his round of lamp lighting duties.

The sudden burst of fire in the darkening inn had caught Rogo's eye as he stood behind the bar counter polishing the glass. He watched as Stumpy's prompt action saved the dwarf's beard - and probably the common room from bursting into a brawl that would once more wreck the furniture. Rogo nodded to himself with satisfaction for the way his helper had handled the situation and resumed the glass cleaning.

He had been cleaning the glass for some time. In fact that's all he did with it. No one in their right minds would put a glass out on the tables of the common room. It would be broken in seconds - probably into someone's face. But Zama wanted the occasional passing traveller who happened into their inn to know that it was a place of quality. That's why Rogo was cleaning the glass. And, as well as impressing the gullible, it was always handy to smash into the face of anyone trying to make off with the cash box. And while he stood cleaning the glass he could look around the common room.

As he did there was nothing unusual for him to see. The gang from the castle slept on. the mysterious traveller who arrived breathlessly a few hours earlier was relaxing over his second tankard while picking at the few scraps he'd still got left on his platter, the two "priests of Elna" were in deep conversation with another newcomer to the region and Skutlar still sat slumped at the counter.

Rogo paused once more in his glass wiping watching the priests of Elna. It was not going to go well for the newcomer. Someone was going to have to do something before this potential source of steady income for the inn ended up on some sacrificial altar or other. "This is a job for the militia," thought to himself and looked around for the duty officer who should be positioned within the inn. Then he realised that it was Skutlar. Face down on the counter there wasn't going to be a lot he was going to do. Where was a hero when you needed one? Then he remembered that he had sent them off to rescue that 'king'. "Well," he thought to himself, "I guess it's down to me."

As he reached under the counter for his trusty club the door of the tavern burst open. Light from the setting sun reflected from the windows of the cottages on the opposite side of the road and dazzled anyone who happened to look in that direction. Suddenly that light was obscured as a troll or possibly a small hill giant - to judge by its silhouette - moved through the open doorway and into the common room. Rogo relaxed. His silent request had been answered. He recognised Thrugg as he strode into the common room.

To all and sundry the triumphant hero announced the obvious. "We have returned," he bellowed. The patrons gathered in the various shadowy corners of the inn reacted to the announcement in a variety of different ways.

The dwarf sleeping on Markenbrat's left suddenly sat bolt upright and announced that he would drink to that. His fellow workers sleepily agreed, lifted their tankards still full of stale ale to their lips, drained them and resumed their slumbers. At the same table Malifest opened his eyes and immediately wished he hadn't. He peered across the common room and recognised the man mountain Thrugg. Still clutching his finely crafted silver goblet full of a dark green liquid that was smoking he gingerly rose and crossed to greet his friend. The journey did him no good at all. By the time he reached the warrior Malifest was as green as the contents of his goblet. He turned to Rogo. "Take this," he instructed the inn keeper, " and whatever I say don't give it me back!" With that the elven prince on his mission to try and understand ordinary people fled through the front door. The exit was followed by the sound of retching as the elf was made to feel suddenly a lot better.

The "priests of Elna" were clearly overjoyed to see the return of the key members of the Sham militia returning to their station. They were eager to carry the news to their brother priests who at this sunset hour were sure to be gathering in the nearby woods. They left in a rush to join them, completely forgetting about the newcomer who they had spent quite some time and not an inconsiderable amount of money persuading to join their order for the service. Only Rogo noticed that they turned right out of the inn door and not left. If you were heading for the Elna gathering place you would turn left, particularly if you were anxious to get there. Turning right meant you were heading for the Mayor's place - but the Mayor was in the tavern - or the pawn brokers which was closed or the Temple dedicated to the little blue god Kalaar. "Just as I thought," Rogo reflected, making a mental note to sort out those "Elna priests" if ever they came back to his inn.

No one could really see how the mysterious stranger reacted, sitting as he was in one of the dimly lit corners of the common room. It would have taken the sharpness of elf vision to penetrate that gloom. At present the nearest elf was still inspecting the recent contents of his stomach as he lent against the horse trough just outside the inn. However, if he had been inside the inn and looking in the right direction he would have seen a wry smile cross the stranger's lips. Then he settled himself more at ease on his chair before reaching to sip a little more of his post dinner drink. Something had amused him about the adventurer's return but he was keeping that secret to himself.

Skutlar reacted to Thrugg's bellow by groping along the bar until his fingers found his mug. He brought it to his lips and drunk some of the contents. He sighed and once more became the immobile bar ornament known so well. "All without opening his eyes and barely lifting his head," commented Gertrude who had followed Thrugg into the room. Rogo did a quick head count and smiled with genuine pleasure that all his friends had returned. He was now able to conduct a more detailed examination, assessing the wounds and other signs that would reveal how difficult the journey had been. He couldn't help but notice the bulging sacks that each of the adventurers carried.

"And not without some gain I see," he responded to Thrugg's initial announcement. "Let see what you've got," he added. At once Thrugg and Gertrude emptied their sacks onto the bar counter. Treasure of all sorts spilled out. Soon more had been added by the others and Rogo's eyes shone with the potential of it all. After a suitable pause to give the impression of assessing it's worth he started "Well, it doesn't look as if I can advance you very much for this load of ..." before Eldon cut him off.

"Rogo," he interrupted, " let's do it the other way. Much as I enjoy the haggle - which I inevitably lose - we're tired. It's been a long, hard, couple of days. Why don't you just provide an accurate assessment and keep 1 bean in 10 for all your trouble?"

With a nod Rogo's mind went into overdrive as he complied an inventory of the riches laid before him. Pair of silver goblets, fine quality with engravings of birds, 60 beans the pair; 8 - no 10 - small diamonds drilled to make a necklace, 120 beans; 4 bowls, silver, suitable for holding sweets or other small edibles, 160 beans; assorted plates in silver, pewter and copper, 150 beans the lot; a mixture of orcish ritual magic items worth at least 200 beans and assorted minor jewels, trinkets and other items making a total of: "840 beans plus whatever Mandrake says the magic items and scrolls are worth," he reported.

"That's fine," said Eldon, "But there just one more little collection to look at. Thrugg."

Acknowledging his instructions Thrugg said "I'm sorry Gerald" before reaching down and grabbing the scout's ankles. In an instant Gerald found himself dangling over the bar counter being shaken vigorously. Small item after small item fell from concealed pockets add to the haul. Once the rain of treasure had come to an end Thrugg carefully returned the chest fallen and chastised scout to his feet.

Surveying the newly appeared items Rogo asked, looking directly at Gerald, "Is that everything?". "Of course," Gerald answered but the twinkle in his eye told a different story. Rogo sighed so as to hide the smile that was forming on his lips and did some more mental arithmetic and announced "That makes an even 1000 beans plus the magic items then. Shall I credit it to your account, less my commission of course?"

Receiving nods of confirmation from Eldon and the others he made a note in his little book before continuing: "But there's just a couple of items missing. First I hired you one of my largest sacks of cabbages and where's the King?"

"Orcs ate the cabbages," said Thrugg, which for him was quick thinking, before Eldon continued with " ... and about the king? That's a long story and best told over a drink."

Always we an eye for a profit Rogo said "O.K. Why don't I put this lot over here and buy you lot your usuals? Go and sit with that traveler - I'm sure he'd be impressed with your tales - and I'll bring them over." Eldon was eager to seize this opportunity to boast about his exploits to a stranger, which was exactly what Rogo had intended. The warrior puffed up his chest, squared his shoulders, drew himself up to his full height and led the way to the table in the corner. His band of adventurers followed, Gertrude bringing up the rear.

Before leaving the bar counter she paused and turned back to look at her inn keeper friend. "Rogo," she cautioned, " You will remember that I know everything that we put on the counter won't you and Zama wouldn't like it if any of it went missing before she had a chance to look it at, would she?" As innocent as a new born baby, or a lamb about to be slaughtered, Rogo replied: "Why, Gertrude, I'm surprised you even suggested it. That was the furthest thing from my mind. " Which, of course, it wasn't.

Chapter 11: The Never Ending Pursuit

Approaching the dark stranger sitting in shadows Eldon paused. He looked at the dim shape and wondered if he would resent the intrusion. He coughed quietly and the stranger turned his head to look at him. Eyes met eyes and Eldon felt that he was drowning in the dark pools before him. There was a pause that from Eldon's point of view lasted an eternity. Eventually the stranger spoke: "Well?". The single word was laden with menace and might have been carved in stone. As might have Eldon for all the reaction it received from him.

Standing just behind their leader Gertrude hissed into Gerald's ear: "He'll be doing his goat impression again if we're not quick!" With a smile and a nod the scout stepped in to rescue their leader - and not for the first time. "Rogo said we were to join you," he explained.

Now Gerald was the focus of the black pools. He took the attention better than his leader had, disarming the stranger with his usual casual smile. The stranger turned away and once more lifted his drink to his lips. "It's his inn," he said to no-one in particular. Led by Eldon the adventurers seated themselves around the table.

Rogo was not far behind with the tray full of drinks. He served all those sitting at the table - fruit juice for Gertrude, red wine for Quickbeam, ale for Thrugg and Gerald and a sweet sherry for Eldon. He topped up the traveller's drink and was about to sit down when it sounded like a minor explosion had occurred in the back room that served as the kitchen. "Excuse me," Rogo apologised, "It sounds like Stumpy's having a little trouble with tomorrow's lunch. I told him roast Minotaur was a bit ambitious - particularly as he hadn't actually killed the damn thing yet! I better go and sort things out. You just carry on and I'll catch up later."

He headed off towards the noise, pausing only at the bar counter to collect a sword, leaving the adventurers sitting with the mysterious stranger. There was one of those awkward moments where no-one is quite sure what to say. Eldon and Gertrude sipped their drinks with the satisfaction of the end of a day when the job was well done. Gerald was needlessly cleaning his finger nails with a throwing dagger. Quickbeam was once more searching his pockets and pouches, conducting the endless inventory of material components that is the survival routine of all magic users. The stranger was unmoved by all this. He was also unmoved by Thrugg who was staring at him, his drink untouched in his hand. The look on the warrior's face showed that he was desperately trying to remember something. With Thrugg this was probably going to take some time.

In the end it fell to the stranger to break the silence. "Rogo said you might have a tale to tell that would interest me," he said to no-one in particular. Whether it was what he said, or the way that he said it, the penny finally dropped in Thrugg's cavernous mind. "Eldon... ," he started. His leader cut him off before he could go any further.

"Not now Thrugg," he said, "You'll get your turn in a moment. I'll start." Used to following his leaders orders Thrugg was silent. Gerald watching him - and everything really - closely realised that his friend had put down his drink to grasp his sword. "Now," the scout thought to himself, "What has he noticed that I have missed?" Before he could do anything more Eldon started in on his version of the start of their most recent adventure. Gerald's attention switched to hang on his leader's every word. He knew when something was going to be good for a laugh!

"Recently in this noble village of Sham where I have the honour to serve as Magistrate," Eldon began, " the vile crime of King napping occurred. Clearly something had to be done by someone and I assumed this willing band. Luckily we managed to apprehend one of the bandits who was persuaded to lead us to their hideout. The journey was uneventful ... "

Before Eldon could continue the stranger cut in. "Where's your guide now?" he asked. "Surely he should still be with you so as to answer for his crimes?" That stopped Eldon's version of the narrative dead in its tracks. It looked like all that was left for him were the goat impressions. Gerald stepped in to save the day. "Never mind that for now," he said, "Let me tell you how I led the way into the dark."

Attention now switched to the scout as he related his embellished version of the penetration of the deep, dark, bandits lair. Gerald was really a very good story teller. He had to be following his profession. It was one of the rules of the Scouts Guild that you had to be prepared to talk your way out of trouble if the circumstances warranted it. Another was that you had to be able to run very fast when that failed. Nevertheless the scout had his audience in the palm of his hand as they hung on every word. Even those who had been with him on the journey were fascinated by the tale for it bore no resemblance to what had actually happened.

Gerald was in full flow. He was describing how he had overcome the unwelcome attentions of a hydra while only armed with a throwing dagger when the stranger once more interrupted. "Surely you couldn't have had it all your own way," he inquired. Quickbeam stepped in to fill the breach and, in his eyes, save the day.

"That's where I came in," he started, before continuing with a more or less accurate account of the role he played in overcoming the Acid Dogs when Gerald was caught in the trap. He described in graphic detail the anatomy and physiology of the creatures as well as his skillful dissection of their throat. He was about to continue into more fanciful areas of narrative when the stranger spoke once more. "You appear to have suffered injuries, probably due to that encounter. Who took care of those wounds?" he asked.

Now it was Gertrude turn to take up the narrative. She did so reluctantly, sensing that everything was not quite right with the stranger. She was telling herself that he seemed to know more of their story than he should. But her eagerness to join in the self promotion overcame her so she launched into her account of the amazing healing acts she had performed on their travels.

Once her account drew to its natural conclusion the stranger seemed satisfied that he had heard enough. He finished his drink, dropped a few coins onto the table and stood up. "All that was very, very interesting," he said. "I must be off now. Busy day, you know." With an all embracing nod at the rest of the table he made his way out of the inn and into the light of the setting sun.

There was one of those pauses that follow any session of tale telling. Each of those who had had a chance to speak was reflecting on how they could make their version of the events more interesting at the next recounting. Inevitably it was Thrugg that broke the silence. "Eldon?" he asked.

"Yes Thrugg?" came the reply.

"Is it my turn now?"

"Go on, then, if you must," Eldon instructed, "Although I don't see the point of telling your version of the story now that our audience has left." Thrugg thought for a few moments as was his way as he analysed every word that Eldon had said to him. Finally he reached his conclusion: "I don't won't to make things up about what we have done like the rest of you just did. I want to tell you about something I noticed when we sat down. Did you notice the gloves that the stranger was wearing?"

Once more there was a silence as the team thought back over the last few minutes. It was Gerald that got there first. He used the techniques he had learnt in his scout's training to visualise the stranger dropping the coins on the table to pay for his extra drink. He could see the coins landing one by one on the table's surface - he was always interested in money and where it fell. He rewound the scene in his mind to the moment the coins left the hands. No - it wasn't hands - it was gloves - fine black red leather gloves with a particular style of red and white piping. He'd seen those gloves before - and then he remembered where, when and who.

"Luther," he said quietly in conclusion and his companions signified their agreement.

Thrugg, completing the logic chain interrupted while his friends caught up, went on to say "They were black with red and white piping and I think they were the same ones that Luther was wearing."

Having dealt with the Minotaur, Rogo was watching from behind the bar counter as all of a sudden the best adventurers in Sham saw what had been staring them in the face. As one they leapt to their feet and dashed out of the door of the inn. It was clear that this time Luther was not going to get away. But, of course, he already had. Rogo reached under the counter and once more began to needlessly polish the glass.

"That's the nature of things, Skutlar my old friend," he said to the sleeping form draped over the counter. "Adventurers spend all their time risking life and limb going to strange, protected, out of the way, places to seek their fortunes whilst they fail to take full advantage of the opportunities that are there directly in front of them. I mean, I've lost count of the number of time Wolf Godslayer has managed to sell the Capital Road bridge to newcomers to the region. That's real enterprise. And doing it under Zama's watchful gaze, well, that's a real adventure I say! What do you think?"

Skutlar raised his head off the counter. His ale soddened mind realised that Rogo had asked him a question and an answer was required. You could see the wheels turning as he tried to work out what he should say in these circumstances. In the end the answer came: "That'll be fine Rogo," he said, "I'd love another drink."

Reaching for the ale jug off the back bar Rogo thought to himself: "Just like the rest. Single minded to the end!" as he poured another drink for his best customer.

Now you are that bird again. You leave your roost in the corner of the inn where you have watched these most recent events unfold and once more fly outside to look on the inn and the village in which it stands. Evening is fast coming on and many of the cottages are locked and barred for the night. Behind the ill fitting shutters can be seen the lamp light holding back the surrounding darkness. There is still movement and you land on a convenient perch to observe it more closely.

Adventurers, strangely familiar ones in the half light, are desperately searching for something - someone. Up and down the main street they go, looking in every conceivable hiding place. But nowhere can their quarry be found. You know that it won't be long now before common sense prevails and the search will be abandoned in favour of warmth, food and company in the inn.

The villain has escaped and lives to fight another day. The heroes have survived triumphant and will soon once more be ready to search out adventure for profit and reward. What of you? What will you do now? Will you return to the calm and order of the Capital far to the south or will you stay here to savor the taste of adventure?

As you try to work out your answer, the inn sign on which you has chosen to roost swings gently in the evening breeze beneath you. 'The Portly Pixie' it says. 'Beware: Adventures start here' is the hidden message you read - and you know that it is the taking part in those adventures that counts!

Afterword

From 1987 to 2005 there existed in middle England a hidden village known as Sham. It lay on the fringes of a secret region ruled over by the Duke of Chouse. In order to get to the village you didn't have to go through the back of a wardrobe or travel through time and space. It's true that most of the time you had to seek out a set of football changing rooms on a playing field in Coventry or, in later years, make a journey to a sheep farm near Bulkington. But most of the journey was made by the use of your imagination and a willingness to seek adventure.

At the heart of the village lay an inn called "The Portly Pixie". It is rumored that there the ale tasted like orange squash, honeymead was poured out of metal cans and the chille was really special. But the real story about that inn you've already read earlier in this slim volume.

If you want to go there for yourself, I'm afraid it's too late – unless someone has got a very large sum of money. But the village still exists, as do most of the people who lived or visited – even those who only came for a birthday party. For many of us the collective imagination has made the place very real.

You may think you've just finished reading a story. You may think that all those in it have simply been conjured out of the darker recesses of my mind. The truth is much more fantastic. The Moody Blues, in a poem on their Threshold of a Dream album, speak about the moon being a cold hearted orb, ruling the night. It goes on the say that we decide what is right, and what is illusion. This story is true and, if you want, I could introduce you to Gerald, Eldon, Skutlar and most of the others. I'd stay clear of the Priests of "Elna" though, unless you fancy becoming a sacrifice to a small blue god looking very much like a cast iron garden gnome.

To all of you who know me and Sham personally my thanks for the never ending story that is everyday life in Chouse. If you have found yourself in this tale, I hope I've told it true. If not, keep your eyes open for future volumes.

Every Good Wish,

Rogo
Thane of Sham and Innkeeper

Also know as Roger Price

Further information about The Portly Pixie Live Role Playing Centre can be accessed through the website www.portlypixie.co.uk. Alternatively please write to Roger Price, 30 Heritage Drive, Coventry, CV6 6QR.

Coming Soon

Monopoly

Gerald, Eldon and the rest have fallen on hard times. There haven't been any bandits near Sham for ages. So there's been no treasure to recover and trade. And their bank accounts have dwindled away to nothing. Zama has had enough. She wants their tab cleared and wants it cleared now. There's nothing for it. The finest adventurers in the region are going to have to take on some real work.

Luckily there's a trade caravan going the couple of day's journey to neighbouring Battenburgh and offering good money for bodyguards. Looks like a couple of easy days work to clear their debts.

That is until the caravan is attacked ... And Gerald says "Err, lads, there's something I'd better tell you ..."

That's when their next adventure really begins!

Keep your eye on the website for the publication of this book, where you can also register your interest in ordering a copy.

The Portly Pixie
www.portlypixie.co.uk

Printed in Great Britain
by Amazon

57438469R00061